NO HEROES
We Rotten Few
Book 2

Copyright © 2024 by JJ Benham

All rights reserved.

No part of this publication may be reproduced, distributed, or transmitted in any form or by any means, including photocopying, recording, or other electronic or mechanical methods, without the prior written permission of the author and publisher, except in the case of brief quotations embodied in critical reviews and certain other non-commercial uses permitted by copyright law.

This is a work of fiction. Names, characters, businesses, places, events, and incidents are either the products of the author's imagination or used in a fictitious manner. Any resemblance to actual persons, living or dead, or actual events is purely coincidental.

First paperback edition 2024 (ISBN 9798305311204)

Chapter 1

I'm standing in my house, and everything seems perfect.

The living room is filled with people, and a proper British beige buffet sits on a table in the middle of the room—sausage rolls, scotch eggs, sandwiches, and bowls of assorted nibbles. The warm aroma of freshly baked pastry and salted crisps mixes with the scent of my parents' favourite lavender air freshener.

The room is full of people too, more than should fit comfortably, but there's no sense of claustrophobia. My parents are there, smiling at me from the sofa. My dad raises his glass and nods at me, his Scottish accent even in my mind saying, "Proud of you, son."

Michael Robart is there too—my boss—talking animatedly with Sarah. She's laughing at something he said, her smile as bright as I remember, her laughter light and musical, echoing through the room. Deb and Noah are at the table, Noah's mouth full of crisps, Deb nudging him to chew properly. Nick is leaning against the wall, giving me an exaggerated double thumbs up, his grin wide and reassuring.

It's perfect, this little scene. The kind of gathering I'd always hoped for but never quite got around to arranging. I feel a warmth in my chest—comfort, nostalgia, something like peace. The soft hum of chatter, the clinking of glasses, the crunch of crisps underfoot—it all feels so wonderfully mundane, so blissfully normal.

I pick up a plate and start filling it with food, a sausage roll here, a scotch egg there. I take a bite, the buttery pastry crumbling in my mouth, the savoury flavour of sausage filling my senses. It's all so normal, so plain. I move around the room, chatting with my parents, laughing at one of Michael's jokes, even teasing Noah about stuffing too much food into his mouth. He giggles, bits of crisp falling from his lips, and Deb shakes her head with an exasperated smile. Everyone is happy, everyone is safe.

I catch Nick's eye, and he grins at me, raising his glass in a silent toast. I smile back, feeling a genuine sense of ease. This is what I've always wanted—a moment of normalcy, of family and friends gathered together, no worries, no fears. Just… life. I take another bite, the familiar taste grounding me in this comforting reality.

I wander over to the sofa, settling beside my parents. My mum reaches over, patting my knee affectionately, her hand warm and soft. "It's so lovely to have everyone here, isn't it, Jack?" she says, her voice gentle, filled with that motherly warmth that always made everything feel okay.

"Yeah, Mum, it really is," I reply, my voice thick with emotion I can't quite place. I lean back, letting the sounds of the room wash over me—the laughter and the faint music playing in the background. It all feels so right.

Sarah walks over to me, her smile warm as she reaches out, her hand resting on my arm. There's something in the way she looks at me, something that makes my chest tighten. She's acting like we're still together, her fingers lightly brushing against mine like they used to. A pang of confusion hits me. We're not together anymore. Why is she acting like this?

I look around the room, my gaze landing on Amanda. She's standing near the buffet table, watching everyone with a curious expression, her dark eyes scanning the room as if she doesn't quite belong. That's when it hits me—Amanda *doesn't* belong here. She's not part of this past life, not someone who would be in this kind of scene. My stomach twists, and I feel a creeping unease, the realisation that something is very wrong.

The warmth I felt begins to fade, replaced by a cold, gnawing dread. I look back at Sarah, her smile still there but now it seems wrong, almost forced. Her fingers tighten around my arm, and I try to pull away, but my body doesn't respond. The room feels different now, the air thicker, harder to breathe, as if an invisible weight is pressing down on my chest.

Then, a light. Sickly, yellow, almost orange, starts seeping through the curtains. It's wrong, that light, like it doesn't belong in this world. It casts long shadows that twist and writhe, making the room feel smaller, the walls inching closer. The warmth in my chest curdles, turning into something colder, something that makes my skin prickle. I am reminded of another dream I had, one where I was high above the world, gazing up at a dreadful eye that looked down on us with unreadable malice.

The people start to change. My dad's smile drops, his skin taking on a pallor, his eyes hollowing out, the life draining from his face. Sarah's bright laughter fades, her face sagging, her hair falling in clumps, her eyes empty and staring. Deb's trying to pull Noah back, but his skin is sloughing off, revealing bone, and his wailing fills the room, high-pitched and agonising. Nick's eyes are sunken, and he's pointing at me now, not with a thumbs up, but accusingly, his mouth opening in a silent scream.

The air fills with the rancid stench of rot, a sickly sweetness that turns my stomach, and all at once, they're all decaying, their wails blending together into an agonising chorus. The food on the table turns black, mould growing over it in fast motion, the once inviting aroma replaced by the putrid stench of death and decay, overwhelming my senses.

I try to move, but my legs are rooted to the spot. My eyes dart around, trying to find some way out, but the light is everywhere, the walls are closing in, and the faces—their faces—are melting, twisted, lost, their hollow eyes fixed on me.

I need to wake up. I need to wake up now.

And just like that, I do. My eyes snap open, my heart hammering against my ribs, my skin clammy with sweat. I'm on the floor in the bedroom of a small village house. The curtains are drawn, but there's no sickly light, just the grey pre-dawn filtering through.

I take a deep breath, trying to shake off the feeling of dread clinging to me like a second skin. It was just a dream, but it felt too real, too vivid. I rub my eyes and sit up, glancing over to see Amanda still asleep, her breathing soft and steady.

The silence of the room wraps around me, only broken by Amanda's soft breathing. The echoes of the dream still cling to me, leaving a hollow feeling in my chest. I breathe in deeply, trying to steady my heart, but the smell of lavender lingers in the air—I hate lavender. The thought flashes through my mind, and it takes a moment to push away the dissonance from the dream.

I need to move. I push the blanket away and slowly sit up from the floor, my feet pressing against the cool wooden boards. The morning light creeping through the curtains is pale, giving the room a washed-out look. Everything feels heavy, like I'm still dragging some part of the nightmare with me.

I glance at Amanda, still curled up beneath her blanket, her face softened by sleep, her breaths slow and even. A part of me envies her. Another part wonders if she's haunted by her own nightmares. We've barely talked about what happened to her before I found her—or about what she saw in those first days. Maybe it's easier to keep the horrors unspoken, locked away somewhere deep inside.

I stand up, wincing as my body protests. Every muscle feels stiff, the bruises from the scuffle with that lunatic yesterday making themselves known, my face still throbbing from his boot. I flex my fingers, feeling the stiffness in my knuckles. It's almost funny, in a morbid way—the dead are up and walking yet the living have posed the most danger to me so far. I step quietly to the window and peek through the curtains. The street outside is empty, the sky a dull grey, the kind of sky that promises more rain. Everything is wet from last night's downpour, puddles reflecting the dismal sky, and the world feels utterly still.

A deep breath. I need to keep moving. Amanda and I need to keep moving. Staying in one place is dangerous—the undead are bad enough, but the people, the other survivors… I've learned that lesson well enough. I let the curtain fall back into place and glance around the room seeing if there is anything useful. Nope, nothing. At least I have my bags downstairs I suppose. Enough to keep us on our feet until we find somewhere safer. Here I am assuming she's going to come with me. I don't know that; I haven't even asked her yet.

I look back at Amanda again. She deserves a few more minutes of sleep. I slip out of the bedroom, my steps careful, trying to avoid any creaking floorboards as I head downstairs. The smell of the place hasn't changed—damp mixed with the faint, lingering coppery tang of blood. I grimace, remembering the mess I had to drag out into the garden last night. A cold shiver runs through me. I think I'm starting to get used to it, and that terrifies me.

In the kitchen, I fill the kettle and set it to boil. The mundane action grounds me, the kind of thing I'd done a thousand times before all of this. Just making a cup of tea—something normal, something human. I lean against the counter, listening to the kettle rumble as it heats up, my mind wandering back to the dream. I try to shake it off, but it sticks with me—the way they looked at me, the way they decayed in front of me. My parents, Sarah, Nick…

The whistle of the kettle brings me back to the moment, and I take it off the heat, pouring the hot water into a chipped mug I found in the cupboard. As the tea steeps, I hear the soft creak of footsteps on the stairs. Amanda appears in the doorway, her hair messy from sleep, eyes still a little bleary.

"Morning," she says, her voice barely above a whisper.

"Morning," I reply, offering a small smile. I gesture to the kettle. "Want a cuppa?"

She nods, moving to sit at the small table by the window. "Yeah, thanks." She rubs her eyes, then looks at me. "Did you sleep okay?"

I pause, considering lying, then shake my head. "Not really. Bad dreams." I busy myself with making her tea, not wanting to meet her gaze. I can feel her eyes on me though, and there's something comforting about it—that silent understanding.

"Yeah. Me too," she says after a moment, her voice barely audible.

I turn and set the mug in front of her, our eyes meeting for just a second before we both look away.

There's nothing more to say about it. We're both haunted, and that's just the way it is.

"Listen, I need to get moving soon," I say, taking a sip of my tea, the warmth spreading through me, pushing away the chill that's settled in my bones.

"Where to?" Amanda asks, her voice a little stronger now.

"South," I reply. "My parents' farm… if it's still there." It's a slim hope, but it's all I've got.

She nods, her fingers wrapped around the mug, her eyes thoughtful. "Oh yeah, I remember you mentioning it. South it is then."

A smile forces its way across my face and I try my hardest to repress it. "You're coming with me?"

She smiles at me softly before taking a sip of her tea. That's reply enough for me.

We sit in silence for a few moments, sipping our tea, listening to the rain starting to patter against the window again. It's a small comfort—a quiet moment before we have to face the world outside.

Chapter 2

The morning air is damp as we step out of the house, the lingering chill wrapping around us. The rain has eased up, but the sky remains a heavy, oppressive grey, thick clouds promising that this is just an interlude rather than the end. Amanda and I stand on the narrow cul-de-sac for a moment, taking in the silence of the village. Everything is still, almost unnaturally so, save for the occasional rustle of wind through the trees.

Only now can I take in the street. It's only small, curving off to my left to a dead stop. I know I'm in a relatively wealthy area as these houses are all detached with rather large plots each. Three of the houses have boats on trailers in their drives and one has a huge, very expensive-looking caravan of sorts.

"Any idea where we should start?" Amanda asks, her voice quiet but carrying in the otherwise dead silence.

"This is your village, not mine," I say, glancing back at her as she shuts the front door behind her.

"Jack, you're more of a local than I am up here," she says, smiling. "I'm from London."

"Oh… of course you are, your accent, how bloody obvious." I shake my head, feeling a bit foolish.

Amanda chuckles softly, and I can't help but smile back. Despite everything, her humour helps to cut through the grim reality we find ourselves in, if only for a moment.

"Alright, then," I say, looking around. "Let's head further in, see if we can find a car we can use. We need to get moving if we're going to make any real progress today."

Amanda nods, adjusting her backpack and falling in step beside me. The road is littered with small debris—branches from last night's storm, scattered rubbish, even a few abandoned bags. As we move further into the village each step echoes too loudly in the silence. My senses are on edge, scanning every doorway, every window, for movement. The feeling of being watched seems to have settled over me, perhaps lingering from my dream.

We pass by a few houses, keeping our eyes peeled for any signs of life, either undead or otherwise. The village is eerily still. No moans, no sounds of shuffling feet—nothing to indicate the presence of anything at all. It's unsettling. I'd rather hear them and know where they are than be left with this strange silence. To be so close to the M6 and it be this soundless triggers something deep in my brain, giving me this foreboding sense of dread, as if my body knows this is all wrong.

We reach a small crossroads. There's a pub to our left, the windows dark, the door slightly ajar. I hesitate, staring at the entrance. Places like that—they make me uneasy now. Too many nooks and crannies, too many shadows for something to be hiding in. Amanda follows my gaze and gives me a questioning look.

"Should we check it out?" she asks, her voice hushed.

I shake my head, pushing down the fear building in my gut at the idea of going inside. "Not worth it. We're better off sticking to the plan."

She nods, and we move on, leaving the pub behind. The road starts to widen, and we find ourselves in what must be the village centre. There's a small row of shops—a bakery, a convenience store, a charity shop. A few cars are parked along the street, but none of them look promising. One has its bonnet crumpled in, another's doors are hanging open, like someone had already scavenged what they could before abandoning it. Either that or they fled in a hurry.

"What about that one?" Amanda says, pointing ahead to a small hatchback. It's parked in front of what used to be a florist, the windows intact, and no immediate signs of damage.

We approach cautiously, my grip tightening around the bat in my hand, Amanda's katana ready at her side. I nod to her, and she moves to check the driver's side door, giving the handle a tug. It's locked. Typical.

"Want to break a window?" she asks, raising an eyebrow.

I hesitate, glancing around. The noise could draw attention—attention we don't need. But we might not have a choice. I look inside the car, trying to see if the keys might still be in there. No luck, that would be too easy. "Give me a second," I say, moving around to the back, peering through the rear window. It's empty, save for a couple of reusable shopping bags. "Doesn't look like there's anything useful in there."

Amanda frowns. "Should we keep looking, then?"

I'm about to respond when a noise catches my attention. A scraping sound, like something dragging across the pavement. I freeze, my head snapping towards the source of the sound. Amanda goes still too, her eyes widening as we both listen. The sound grows louder, closer. It's coming from one of the side streets, just out of sight.

I motion for Amanda to get down, and we crouch behind the hatchback, peeking over the bonnet. The scraping continues, and soon enough, we see it—an undead, its leg twisted at an unnatural angle, dragging itself along the street. It hasn't noticed us yet, its blackened eyes staring blankly ahead as it shuffles forward, one arm reaching out with each lurching step.

I glance at Amanda, and she gives me a nod, her expression set. We can't let it spot us; I know that but I feel my legs tighten as if setting in concrete. My palms begin to sweat, slickening my tight grip on the handle of my bat. Turns out I've not gotten used to this, and I don't think I ever will.

Amanda looks at me, waiting. I swallow hard, my heart pounding, and step out from behind the car. My legs feel heavy, my arms like lead. I raise the bat, but my muscles lock, the weight of everything I've seen, every failure, bearing down on me. Memories flood in—Nick's face, the blood, the screams—all the times I hesitated, all the times I couldn't act. My heart thunders in my ears, drowning out everything but the fear. The zombie turns towards me, its vacant eyes locking onto mine, and it lets out a low, haunting wail as if the man he once was is trapped inside this creature. My breath catches, my hands trembling as I try to force myself to move, to do anything—but I can't. I'm frozen, helpless, stuck in the ever-growing familiarity of icy terror.

Why are we even doing this. It might have just walked on by, not noticed us. No. I'm sure it would have.

Suddenly, Amanda is there. Her katana arcs through the air, slicing clean through the creature's neck. It crumples to the ground, the mournful groan cutting off abruptly. Amanda turns to me, her eyes filled with understanding, a mix of urgency and sympathy.

"It's okay, Jack," she says softly, her voice grounding me, pulling me back from the edge. "Let's keep moving."

I force a shaky smile, wiping my sweating hands on my trousers.

We continue down the street, our eyes peeled for anything useful—a vehicle, supplies, anything that might give us an edge. The further we go, the more apparent it becomes that this village, like everywhere else, has already been picked over. Windows are shattered, doors hang open, and anything of value has no doubt been taken. The entire time we search I feel watched, expecting threats to come round every corner or through broken windows. So, this is stress. I smile to myself, a weak attempt to make light of my deeper concerns.

With all the signs of human activity, we are yet to see anyone. No survivors and only the one dead guy. Where the hell is everybody? It's almost as if the village up and vanished overnight.

Eventually we come across a small garage, the kind that might have once serviced the local cars in the village and not much else. The large door is partially open, and I exchange a glance with Amanda. "Worth a look?" A question I so desperately want her to say no to.

She nods. I swallow my discomfort as we approach cautiously, ducking under the half-open door. It's dark inside, the smell of oil and rust thick in the air. There's a car on the lift, an old estate that looks like it hasn't run in years. Tools are scattered across the floor, and a workbench lines one wall, cluttered with odds and ends I couldn't possibly try to identify.

Amanda moves towards the bench, picking through the tools, while I check the car. It's a mess, the interior torn apart, the engine exposed. No way this thing is going anywhere. I let out a frustrated sigh, stepping back.

"Jack," Amanda calls, her voice hushed. I turn to see her holding something up—a set of keys, a hopeful look in her eyes.

"Where did you find those?" I ask, moving closer.

She gestures to a small pegboard on the wall, the rest of the pegs empty. Makes sense.

"Think they might belong to something here?"

I glance around, my eyes landing on a dusty SUV parked in the corner, half-hidden beneath a tarp. It looks old, but not beyond use. "Only one way to find out," I say, taking the keys from her.

We move over to the SUV, and I pull the tarp away, revealing a beat-up but intact vehicle. The tyres look good, and there's no obvious damage. I exchange a hopeful glance with Amanda before sliding the key into the lock. It turns with a satisfying click, and I open the door, peering inside. It's a little dusty, but otherwise clean. I climb in, sliding the key into the ignition, a heavy thrum filling my chest as I turn it.

For a moment, nothing happens. Then, the engine begins to turn over several times, only serving to heighten my anxiety. After a few seconds that feel eternally longer, the engine rumbles to life, a rough, sputtering growl that fills the garage. I let out a breath I hadn't realised I was holding, a grin spreading across my face. "We've got wheels." That sounded better in my head.

It's a small victory, but it's something. I turn to look at Amanda, still smiling when movement from the far corner of the garage catches my attention. Amanda clearly notices my expression change, eyes widening with mine. The mechanic—undead, eyes dark in the gloom—is barrelling towards her from a small office, his gait uneven but relentless moving at a horrifying jogging pace.

"Amanda!" I shout, my voice cracking with panic.

Before she can react, the mechanic crashes into her, his weight sending them both careening into the side of the SUV. The impact is sickening, metal groaning under the force, and Amanda cries out as she struggles against the undead, her katana pinned between her and the mechanic.

I feel the fear rise, the familiar paralysis trying to take hold, hearing the sounds of the struggle bring back bitter memories of Nigel and his wife. My neighbour who was torn apart because I couldn't act. I can hear his voice in my head blending with Amanda's cries for help and her strains to keep the mechanic's gnashing jaws at bay.

I clench my eyes shut, the icy grip of terror—my old friend—tightening its hands around me, bidding me to remain silent, safe.

In the darkness behind my eyelids, I see a face for a brief moment—Nick. How? The apparition brings clarity fourth, a realisation that my cowardice has already cost the lives of my neighbours. I won't allow it to consume the lives of anyone else. The vision of Nick spurs me on like the summer warmth banishing the winter cold.

I pull on the door handle and ram the door into the mechanic's head with all of my strength. The impact is foul, a sickening, wet thud followed by him sprawling off Amanda and to the side.

Amanda scrambles to her feet, her breathing ragged. She grabs her katana and without a moment's hesitation, drives it into the mechanic's head but her strength—all but sapped from her—faulters and the blade fails to pierce the skull, instead sliding off to the side.

I hear her gasp, a sound she may as well have made for the both of us. That warmth I felt just moments earlier bids me forward and I leap from the car, bat raised and ready.

The mechanic shambles to his feet releasing a low growling groan that seems to vibrate the stuffy air within the garage. There is a hint of frustration, but that could just be me imagining things. His face is now more horrifying. A large flap of flesh hangs loosely to one side, the result of Amanda's failed strike. I can see the white bone beneath the gore and the sight threatens to expel the contents of my stomach.

A flash of memory springs into my mind as I ready myself. 'Blunt weapons are far more effective against the undead'. A quote from one of the myriad zombie books I have read or listened to over the years. Weirdly it instils a confidence within me.

The mechanic rushes forward on uneven legs, its head bobbing awkwardly. I move quickly to meet his advance, bringing the bat upwards swiftly. The sound the bat made when it connected with the zombie's chin will not be something I soon forget. The undead mechanic with his blue overalls is sent backwards two or three steps but before it can recover, I close the distance swinging the bat violently.

With two more cracks of the bat, he goes down in a tangled heap of limbs and blood. I stand over my kill, my chest heaving as adrenaline courses through me still. I stare down at his open skull and feel nothing but anger. A short-lived moment ruined by an unstoppable wave of vomit that washes any courage from me. I keel over and throw up onto the body. Not my finest moment and sadly one that was witnessed in its entirety by Amanda.

Not wanting to dwell on the embarrassment, my mind wanders. Where did that come from? I had tunnel vision like never before. I felt almost... possessed. The fact I just did that, acted like that sends a deep chill along my spine and my mind struggles to come to terms with it.

At the same time, I liked it. But I also hated it.

Amanda stands there for a moment, her chest rising and falling as she catches her breath, all the while staring at me with a shocked expression.

"You, okay?" I manage to say, my voice now shaky.

Amand, still staring replies with an unsteady voice. "Yeah... yeah, I'm fine." She wipes her forehead with the back of her hand, her gaze shifting to the SUV.

"Thanks, Jack. Where did that come from?"

"I don't really know..." I say, electing not to mention Nick.

"Well thank you," she says, a serious expression on her face.

I nod, swallowing the lump in my throat. The fear is still there, the self-doubt, but maybe—just maybe—I'm not entirely useless. "Let's get out of here," I say, my voice steadier now.

Amanda gives me a nod, and we both climb into the SUV after collecting my bags. I adjust the seat, my hands trembling slightly as I grip the wheel, the effects of adrenaline wearing off. Amanda settles in the passenger seat, her katana resting across her lap.

I take a deep breath, letting it out slowly. The engine is running, and we have a way out. It's enough for now. I shift the car into gear, and we pull out of the garage, the tires crunching over the debris-strewn pavement.

We drive in silence for a while, the village slowly receding behind us. The roads are oddly empty and the landscape bleak under the oppressive grey September sky. I keep my eyes on the road, my mind still reeling from everything that just happened, everything that *has* happened.

Chapter 3

The drive south is slow, far slower than I'd hoped for and we haven't made the kind of progress I had expected. The motorway stretches ahead, a grey ribbon of tarmac surrounded by open fields with the sky above as overcast as ever. Amanda and I sit in silence, our eyes scanning the horizon, my hands gripping the steering wheel tighter than necessary. Every distant sound, every slight movement, draws my attention—the same lingering paranoia that seems to have settled over me since my dream this morning.

We're still on the M6, and the absence of other vehicles on the road for the last few miles only adds to the unease settling in my stomach. It's too quiet. That oppressive silence, like the village we left earlier, reminds me that the undead aren't the only danger—it's the unpredictability of everything around us. The only upside is that we're now making good pace, not having to weave and dodge around abandoned cars and lorries. In all of my books and movies about zombie apocalypses, the motorways are the worst places to be; cars bumper to bumper blocking all lanes, the undead still belted into their seats. The decision to use the M6 of all motorways was a moment of sheer stupidity in hindsight, but it's been okay so far. Anyway, the last pileup I saw diverted my path into Amanda. Maybe there was some luck in that.

"What are you smiling at?" Amanda asks, her eyes catching mine, and I realise I've been looking at her for too long, lost in thought.

Shit.

"Ah, nothing," I say, turning back to the road, trying to shake off the awkwardness. "Daydreaming, is all."

"Right, daydream while looking at the road then, yeah?" she says, chuckling.

The sound of her laughter brings warmth, something so damn welcome and comforting in this new world. It's the kind of warmth that makes me want to close my eyes, to remember this moment, to cling to it. Guilt follows almost immediately though. Sarah's laughter never did that for me, not in that way. I swallow hard, glancing at Amanda. She's still smiling, oblivious to the turmoil in my head. My mind seems to bounce wildly to old memories now. To things I haven't thought about in years. I'm not a fan.

"How far do you think we'll get?" Amanda asks, and I hope she hasn't noticed how my mind has wandered again.

I cough, trying to sound nonchalant. "Uh, not sure. Looks pretty clear, so hopefully a good few miles." I make a show of scanning the horizon, wanting to sound and look like I know what I'm doing. I catch a flicker of something in her expression, maybe curiosity, before she turns away.

We travel a few more miles in silence, and I can't help but feel weight in it, the heaviness of the unspoken truths and each other's lives we know nothing about. I want to say something, anything, but I'm stuck. Every time I think of a topic, it just dies on my tongue. Maybe she hates me. Maybe she's angry I froze when the mechanic lunged at her. I did act but too late? I blink, trying to push away these unfounded thoughts. I can't afford to get wrapped up in what she may or may not think about me. I need to focus. I need to get us to safety.

The SUV jolts suddenly, hitting something on the road. My heart jumps, my focus snapping back, and I slow down, squinting at the debris now littering the motorway ahead—suitcases, clothes, pieces of plastic and metal—remnants of accidents. Amanda and I exchange a glance, the unease building inside me. It's one thing to be alone out here, but this mess means people were here and it only serves to remind me that other people do actually still exist. The bruises I currently sport are evidence enough of that.

A flicker of pain hits me. Nick's face flashes before my eyes, and I tighten my grip on the wheel. I must have let something slip onto my face, because I caught Amanda watching me.

"I'm fine," I say, forcing the words out, trying to sound more certain than I feel, trying to pre-empt her questions.

She just nods, looking back to the road. We round a slow curve, and then I see it—a wall of vehicles stretched across all lanes, a massive, chaotic pile-up. My stomach sinks.

"Is that…?" Amanda's voice trails off.

"A pile-up. Yeah." I let out a sigh. Of course, it's a pile-up. What else could it be?

"So far so good, huh?" Amanda says, trying for lightness, but I hear the frustration beneath it.

I bring the car to a stop a few metres away from the nearest car in the pile-up and exhale. "I'm just going to take a look," I say, trying to sound like I have a plan. I open the door, the cold air hitting me, and step out. I scan the road around us, checking for movement, before I make my way over to the SUV's side.

Amanda watches me with a worried expression. "Be careful, Jack," she says.

I nod, climbing onto the roof. The metal is cold beneath my fingers, slick with the damp of the late morning. I pull myself up, standing cautiously. The view ahead makes my stomach churn.

As far as I can see, the motorway is a scene of desolation. Cars are packed in tight, bumper to bumper, filling the entire expanse of asphalt. Vehicles of all kinds—hatchbacks, SUVs, lorries—are wedged side by side, some crooked across lanes, others nudged up against the barrier. There's barely any space between them—it's a solid mass of metal interspersed with wrecks and carnage.

Broken glass glitters in the light, and doors hang open. Clothes, toys, bags, and litter are scattered across the tarmac, remnants of lives now lost. The wind rustles through, lifting light bits of litter into the air, making them drift over the cars like ghosts.

I realise my thoughts have become morbid. Exaggerated, like some gothic poet. My mind often did this, to move to the extreme end of depressing when confronted with a terrible truth.

I remember the day I found out my Grandad had died. I was asked to say a few words at the funeral and I spouted some dark eulogy that utterly crushed the tone of the day. Several members of the extended family refused to speak to me after that day. Not something I was overly bothered by if I'm honest. I wonder if any of them are still alive, surviving somewhere out there, beyond this motorised graveyard.

I spot a few undead meandering between the cars, their movements aimless but unsettling. They wander along the narrow paths left between the vehicles, occasionally bumping into a bonnet or pressing their decaying hands against a window, leaving dark smears across the glass. Their clothes are tattered, flapping loosely as they stagger forward, their hollow black eyes staring blankly, oblivious to everything except some vague sense of movement or sound.

Three quick bangs on the roof beneath my feet make me jump. "So? How's it look?" Amanda calls out.

I climb down off the roof and land on her side of the car and gesture for her to wind the window down. The sight of her bobbing up and down as she hurried to wind the window using the old school crank handle was amusing but did little to cheer my mood.

"Shit," I mutter. "We're on foot from here it seems."

Amanda lets out a sigh, her eyes following the line of cars ahead. "Great. Just what I always wanted." She glances at me, a small smile playing on her lips. "Guess it's good exercise, though."

I shake my head, a forced smile tugging at my own lips. "Yeah, just what we need. Come on, let's grab what we can carry."

Amanda pulls her backpack from the backseat while I grab mine and a few additional supplies—water bottles, a first aid kit, whatever we might need. My mind wanders to Nick again; I wouldn't have any of this if it wasn't for him. I take a deep breath, glancing up and down the motorway, looking for any signs of movement besides the shambling dead.

Amanda adjusts her bag, her eyes scanning the horizon. "How far do you think we'll need to go before we find a break in this mess?"

"No idea. Could be a mile, could be ten." I give her a weary shrug. "We'll just have to see how it goes. At least it's still daylight."

She seems lost in her own thoughts for a moment, her gaze distant. I watch her, concerned. "You, okay?" I ask.

"…Yeah," she says, snapping out of her momentary lapse. "Do you think it's happened everywhere?"

I smile involuntarily, the question catching me off guard. There's something almost comforting in the familiarity of it.

"What are you smiling at?" she asks, her face serious.

"Sorry, it's just… that's always the question, isn't it? It's always asked in the zombie books and movies; one character always asks."

Amanda raises an eyebrow, clearly judging me. "Come on, you've seen movies surely? Whenever some apocalyptic event happens, someone always asks that same question."

Eventually, her eyebrow lowers, and she half smiles. "Yeah, I suppose that's true. Very sorry I'm the cliché!" She laughs.

"To answer though, I'm not sure. I hope not."

To the left side of the motorway lies a wooded area, fairly thick and stretching off into the distance. My body gives me warning signs at the idea of walking through the sea of abandoned vehicles. I know there are dead in there. I can't look everywhere at once, and all it takes is one mistake for me to become one of them. Having Amanda at my side is a blessing, but she can't protect me all the time, and vice versa.

We both approach the first of the cars, and the weight of the cricket bat in my hands fails to comfort me. A knot tightens within my core, anxiety and fear welling up, urging me to find another way. Almost instinctively, my gaze shifts toward the woods once more.

"Think we should walk in there?" I say, pointing to the trees just off to the side.

Amanda follows my finger before turning back to me. "No. I don't."

"It's better than walking through this metallic graveyard," I say, gesturing to the pileup ahead. "I don't want to get grabbed through an open window. At least in there, there are fewer places for them to hide," I say, my voice almost pleading.

She pauses for what feels like an eternity before she speaks. "Fine. But let's stay close together, and keep your eyes open. They all could have wandered in there from the road."

The wave of relief that washes over me is indescribable. Something deep inside me is telling me not to walk among the cars. Call it a sixth sense, intuition, whatever you want, but I'm just glad Amanda agreed and that we don't have to; that I don't have to.

Amanda and I move toward the edge of the woods, the damp earth giving way beneath our feet as we step off the asphalt. The air shifts immediately—it's quieter here, the noise of the wind muffled by the thick canopy above. The trees stand tall and close together, their branches intertwining, creating a tangled roof that blocks much of the grey sky above. The ground is littered with broken twigs, and each step we take sends small rustles echoing into the stillness.

"Watch your footing," Amanda says quietly, her eyes scanning the undergrowth. She moves with a sense of ease, her katana held low at her side, her eyes flicking between the woods and the motorway, keeping watch for anything that might follow us.

I nod, swallowing hard as I clutch the cricket bat, my fingers sinking into the rubberised grip. My steps are less certain than hers, my gaze darting between the shadows beneath the trees. I can't help but imagine the dead, lurking just out of sight, waiting for us to make a mistake.

"Think we'll see anyone out here?" I ask, my voice barely above a whisper. It feels wrong to speak too loudly, like we'll draw unwanted attention.

Amanda glances at me, her expression unreadable. "Maybe. If they're smart, they'd avoid the roads too. But who knows. Everyone's desperate now, look at us."

She was right. Look at us. Two strangers brought together by some unthinkable tragedy that spans who knows how much of the world. Desperately trudging through a stretch of woodland just off the M6 to who knows where. As for others, well we'd seen the best humanity could offer. I'd seen more of it than her and I can safely say I don't wish to run into anyone else until I see my parents.

We walk in silence for a while, the crunch of the undergrowth beneath our feet the only sound. The motorway, with its chaos of abandoned vehicles, slowly fades from view, replaced by the endless rows of trees. There's a stillness here, a sense of isolation that's both comforting and terrifying. I'd exchanged the myriad hiding places between parked vehicles for the ominous feeling of a shaded wood. I am beginning to regret my insistence.

Amanda stops suddenly, holding up a hand. I lock up, my hear hammering in my ribcage as I follow her gaze. Ahead of us, a figure moves between the trees—slow, staggering, the telltale gait of the undead. Its head lolls to the side, its arms hanging limply as it shuffles forward, unaware of our presence.

I hold my breath, my grip tightening on the bat. Amanda turns to me, her eyes locking onto mine. She doesn't need to say anything—I know what I have to do, yet a voice in the back of my mind asks, *why me?* My stomach twists, fear clawing at my insides. I take a step forward, the bat feeling heavy in my hands. Another step. The dead thing doesn't react, its back still to us, its ragged clothes hanging from its frame.

As I approach, a sight stops me dead in my tracks. Barely visible behind a nearby tree, shaded under a thicker portion of the canopy, a pale, mottled face watches me, its blackened eyes unblinking.

I freeze, my entire body locking up in the icy grip of fear I've come to know all too well. I know it sees me, but it doesn't react. The first undead continues shambling aimlessly between the trees, seemingly unaware of us. I stand completely still—a statue of fear—but I watch. My body is frozen, but my mind is still active.

My eyes scan the trees around me, and I see them. One, two, three... about a dozen pale corpses standing perfectly motionless beneath the trees, their forms mostly concealed. All staring right at me.

Have they set a trap? Surely not...

The thought sends an even colder chill down my spine, the hairs on my neck standing on end. I watch the first zombie, its movements, its path.

Holy shit...

It's moving in a circle, its eyes always cast down to the ground. *Was that to make us think it hadn't seen us?* My mind is warring with itself now, paranoia seeping in. My rational side tries to debunk the evidence in front of me.

Between the cloud cover and the thick tree canopy, the woods are dark, obscuring their faces. How can I even be sure they're actually looking at me? Maybe it's pareidolia—the mind's tendency to see faces in random patterns.

No. They *are* looking at me. Staring right at me with their black, dead, unblinking eyes. I scan them all again, and this time I see the wounds—one missing an arm, another missing the flesh on part of its face.

How the hell do I get out of this one?

I decide to turn, attempting to be nonchalant, and look back towards Amanda. She's crouching by a tree, her face a picture of confusion. She throws her hands up and shrugs exaggeratedly.

My mind struggles to figure out how to communicate what I see to her without being too obvious to my spectators. I replay scenes from movies where characters silently communicate threats with elaborate hand gestures and signals.

Sod it, I think to myself. I try my best sleight of hand and hold up ten fingers to her, then quickly gesture to some of the concealed figures.

She seems to understand at least part of my message, her eyes narrowing as she scans the woods around us.

Then my heart sinks as I hear a twig snap behind me, back in the direction of the first circling undead. I spin quickly to see it now only five or so steps away, motionless. It's facing away from me, which is good, but the fact that it's stopped moving unsettles me. I look at the other gaunt faces among the trees—they all remain still, staring.

The unsettling stillness gnaws at my mind, and panic begins to rise. I feel it urging me to move, to act, to do something. I feel my body engage, the frozen paralysis from before now gone. My motionless stance is now entirely voluntary. Energy courses through my limbs, almost forcing them to move without my consent.

I turn back to Amanda, who is now looking directly at me with a stern expression. She shrugs again.

"For fuck's sake," I mutter, frustration overtaking the dread and paranoia. I move towards her and crouch by her side.

Her face is filled with concern, her frown ringing in my mind as clarity rushes back to me. I'd gotten so worked up and frustrated that I'd abandoned the safety of feigning ignorance. I look around, listening. No movement. The first undead we'd seen is now shuffling aimlessly again.

"What are you doing?" Amanda whispers, making me jump.

"Sorry, shit, erm... There's like twelve of them just standing in the shadows, hidden behind trees. They were all staring at me," I say, knowing full well how I must sound. I almost refuse to say the next part, but I do anyway. "I think they've set a trap for us..."

Amanda's face is deadpan as she stares blankly into my eyes. She holds that look for maybe three seconds before bursting into a stifled laugh, smothering her mouth with her arm.

"Go away," I say, giving her a gentle shove. I can feel my face heating up again.

"I didn't see any others, Jack. Let's just deal with this one and keep moving," she says after composing herself.

Before I can protest or react, she stands and walks over to the first corpse, taking it out with two swift swings. It didn't even turn around. She makes it look so damn easy. I join her after an uneasy moment of scanning the surroundings once more. Seeing no sign of the ghoulish onlookers, I step up beside her.

"Jack..."

Before I can form a response, the area around us comes alive with the haunting wails of the undead. Twigs snap underfoot, and small bushes part as their forms shamble into view from the shadows.

"I fucking told you," I say to her as we stand back-to-back, readying ourselves.

Chapter 4

Amanda and I spin around, our backs pressed together, the wails of the undead swelling around us. The shadowy figures that had been lurking in the distance now burst forth from the trees, their movements jagged and unnervingly fast. Branches snap, and the soft earth gives way to the relentless advance of decaying feet.

"Jack, move!" Amanda shouts, her voice slicing through the chaos.

I don't need to be told twice. My adrenaline spikes, surging my legs into motion as I swing my bat at the first creature that lunges towards me. The impact reverberates through my arms, the bat connecting with a sickening crunch that sends the ghoul sprawling into the undergrowth. But there's no time to stop, no time to think. The woods are alive with them, and the space between the trees feels like it's shrinking.

Amanda's katana flashes beside me, a swift arc that ends the mindless shrieking of another undead. Her eyes meet mine for a split second, fierce and focused. "We need to find a way out—now!"

My heart pounds, a wild rhythm against my ribs. The narrow path we've carved out is rapidly being consumed by the horde closing in, and every direction seems blocked by snarling, dead bodies. My mind races, scanning for an opening, some sliver of a chance we can slip through. The woods had felt safer, but now the dense trees feel like a deathtrap, every shadow hiding another nightmare. Perhaps we should have gone through the cars after all.

"There!" I shout, pointing to a gap in the trees that looks like it leads to open ground. "Go!"

Amanda doesn't hesitate—she pushes forward, cutting through anything that gets in her way. I follow close behind, my heart in my throat as I hear the snarls getting closer, feel the foul metallic stench of blood and gore clawing at the air around me. I swing the bat again, a desperate backhand that connects with a jaw, shattering bone. I grit my teeth, the panic clawing at the edge of my mind, threatening to swallow me w

Suddenly, Amanda stumbles, her foot catching on an exposed root. She crashes down, her katana slipping from her grip as she hits the forest floor hard. I spin around, the world narrowing to just her and the reaching hands of the undead only feet away. Time seems to slow, my vision tunnelling on her wild eyes. I can see the panic in her eyes, the sheer vulnerability of that moment, the fear contorting her face.

"No!" I yell, adrenaline overriding every ounce of fear. I lunge forward, my bat swinging in wide, desperate arcs. The undead nearest her is knocked off balance, falling to the side with a guttural growl. I drop to my knees beside Amanda, grabbing her arm, hauling her to her feet.

"We have to move!" I shout, pulling her towards the gap, not daring to look back.

Amanda recovers her balance, grabbing her katana and nodding. Together, we push through, breaking into the clearing. For a moment, the open air feels like freedom—but there's no time to celebrate. More undead are coming, bursting from the tree line like a tide of decay, and all we can do is keep running.

The landscape ahead slopes downward, leading to an embankment that drops into a stream. Without thinking, we head for it, the momentum of our escape carrying us forward. Amanda's breath is ragged and shallow beside me, but she doesn't slow. The snarls of the dead are so close behind us now that I can almost feel their bony fingers reaching for my neck.

"Jump!" I yell as we reach the edge of the embankment, and without hesitation, we leap, the ground falling away beneath us.

The cold shock of the stream hits me like a punch, the water freezing as I plunge in, the current sweeping me momentarily off my feet. I surface, gasping, Amanda splashing up beside me, her eyes wide, her face pale but determined. We scramble to the opposite bank, clawing our way up the muddy slope, slipping, our hands digging in for purchase.

As we reach the top, we collapse for a split second, gasping for breath. The sound of the undead is still there, muffled by the water and distance, but growing. I look at Amanda, and she meets my gaze, that fierce determination that was burning in her eyes replaced by something more vulnerable, afraid.

"We keep moving," I say to her, my voice ragged but resolute having found some deep font of strength. "We keep moving, Amanda. We have to."

She nods, forcing herself up with me. My body screams in protest, every muscle aching, but I can't afford to stop. Not now. Not ever. Together, Amanda and I turn away from the chaos behind us, pushing forward into whatever lies ahead—alive, and still fighting.

The adrenaline coursing through my veins is starting to wear off, leaving a dull ache in its place, each step growing heavier, my legs feeling like lead. Amanda's breathing is laboured beside me, and I know she's struggling too.

We stumble through the underbrush, the dense woods slowly thinning out. The trees begin to spread apart, the ground beneath us levelling out, and finally, we reach a small clearing. It's quiet here—eerily so, the only sound our own panting breaths and the rustling of the leaves in the breeze.

Amanda leans against a tree, her face flushed, her chest heaving. I sink down to the ground, my back resting against a rock. For a moment, neither of us speaks. We just breathe, letting the stillness wash over us.

I close my eyes, trying to block out everything, but the memories come flooding back. My hands begin to tremble as I realise that I am terrified. But I didn't lock up. There was no icy terror, no frozen paralysis—just action.

I open my eyes and let out a long sigh of relief. Amanda is looking right at me, her expression neutral, giving no indication of her thoughts.

"Amanda?" I ask, my voice breaking. "Are you okay?"

She doesn't respond with words, just nods slightly. I notice her bottom lip tremble, her eyes watering as she turns away. I feel utterly useless in this moment. I've never been able to comfort anyone in situations like this. Admittedly, I've never been in a bloody apocalypse before, but still, even in normal sad situations, I'm terrible. I always say or do the wrong thing, making it awkward. Do I go over and hug her? I don't even know her. What should I say?

She's facing away from me now, her shoulders bobbing slightly. She's crying. Why shouldn't she? Honestly, I'm amazed I haven't cried yet. This whole zombie outbreak thing isn't going at all how I envisioned it. All those books about normal people becoming heroes on day one—lies. All of it. People aren't as brave as they think they are. I'm living proof of that. Huh, *living*—that's the continuous surprise here.

I'll leave her alone. She doesn't want me bothering her. I stand up, dusting the mud and grime off me, and take a look around. After taking a second to get my bearings, I recognise the direction of the motorway. Definitely don't want to go back that way. In the opposite direction, the trees are sparse and spread apart, and through them, I can just make out the roof of a building or two. Civilisation is good—buildings mean supplies. But… they also mean more zombies, and worse yet, people.

I glance at our bags on the ground next to my blood-splattered bat. We should be okay for now; we've got some first aid supplies, and enough water and food for a few days, I think.

God, this is shit.

I hate having to constantly think about food and water. I miss the convenience of the modern world. Wow, never thought I'd admit that… Maybe I really am losing my mind.

"Jack?" Amanda's voice startles me. She sniffles, turning to look at me, her eyes still red.

"Uh… yeah?" I reply, trying not to look too startled.

"What's the plan? I don't want to stay here too long."

That makes two of us, I think to myself.

"I think I can see some houses over that way," I say, pointing through the trees. "Might be worth taking a look."

She nods, a frail smile tugging at her lips. "Okay."

We walk for five or so minutes until we enter a large, flat field. Beyond it lies a collection of houses—what appears to be another cul-de-sac. Wordlessly, we continue across the field, my eyes scanning the houses ahead. The windows are dark, most obscured by curtains or blinds. Not very helpful.

I spot no movement, and the air is silent except for a gentle breeze. As we approach the end house on the row closest to the field, I notice the telltale signs of a struggle. There's a waist-high fence with a gate leading into the garden. The gate swings softly in the breeze but makes no sound—clearly well-oiled hinges. It's strange what details your brain latches onto in these situations. I'm potentially walking into danger, and I'm thinking about the bloody hinges.

I glance at Amanda. She's focused on the garden, her fingers dancing on the grip of her sword. Her eyes dart around, searching for threats. She looks nervous—no, she looks scared.

I decide not to say anything and move forward toward the gate. In the garden lies a corpse of a man in a dressing gown. His eyes are open, his expression almost peaceful—a stark contrast to the rest of the scene. His chest and stomach are hollowed out, his innards scattered around him, a trail of viscera leading into the open patio doors.

I go to take a step forward, but Amanda stops me, her arm coming across my chest. She turns, her face a mixture of deep concern and sadness.

"What is it?" I whisper.

"Look." She points to the ground, to the trail of blood.

My heart drops into my stomach as I realise what she's pointing at. In the trail of blood, there are multiple sets of footprints. Small ones.

A chill runs up my spine but I elect to ignore the prints for now and focus on the immediate surroundings for any signs of life or… un-life in this case.

My eyes scan the rest of the garden. Beyond the fence in front of us the rest of the house comes into focus—red brick, a steep gable roof, and a dormer window above that peers out like a watchful eye. The patio doors stand open, the curtains inside swaying gently in the breeze. The whole scene feels eerie, like the ordinary suburban life here has been frozen, then shattered.

I look at Amanda again and notice she looks exhausted—emotionally drained. On some level, I think she, like me, wants no part of this house, this street, or whatever village or town this is. My eyes drift down to the little footprints in the blood, and I wonder what it would have been like to die on the first night. Do they know what has happened to them somehow? Some of them wail almost mournfully, as if they're trapped within. No. Stop. I can't think about that. What if my parents have suffered that fate—trapped in their own bodies, cursed to witness every vile deed they do to others. No. I won't accept it.

Amanda puts her hand on my shoulder, bringing me crashing back to reality. I hadn't even realised my mind had wandered so far from where I stand now. The breeze tickles across my face, and I feel wetness on my cheeks. I've been crying. I frown, wiping my face dry, turning away from Amanda in embarrassment.

"Jack, it's normal to be upset," she offers from behind me. "Look around you. None of this is right."

I know she's right, but I need to keep going. Letting myself vanish into my own thoughts like that is dangerous. I can't afford to break down or despair. My weakness has already cost so much, I can't allow it to continue to ruin things. My parents are alive, and I will find them.

"Psst."

My head snaps in the direction of the sound, and I see Amanda tense, anticipating whatever horrors her mind is conjuring. We both wait in silence, our eyes searching around us as we stand motionless.

"Psst, hey!" A hushed voice calls.

Having turned toward the first sound, I manage to spot the source. A young lad is crouching behind the fence of the next house along.

"Hey, what are you—"

"Shh!" he throws back at me before I can finish my sentence. He then beckons us over with one hand, the other pressing a finger to his lips.

Amanda and I exchange a quick look, both of us uncertain. Her eyes narrow, and I see the question there—do we trust this kid? My heart's pounding; we haven't seen another living soul for what feels like forever, and here's this kid, crouched behind a fence like he's playing a game of hide-and-seek. Not to mention that almost everyone else I've run into has ended up being a murderous psycho.

I motion for Amanda to stay put, but she shakes her head. "I'm not letting you go alone," she whispers, her grip tightening on her katana. Maybe she doesn't trust me to handle it, or maybe she just thinks I'll choke again, but I don't argue. At least I know she'll have my back.

"Okay," I whisper, nodding. We move cautiously, staying low as we approach the boy. Each step is careful, our feet avoiding twigs, trying not to make a sound, trying not to attract any attention from whatever might still be lurking nearby. The kid doesn't move an inch, just watches us approach, his wide eyes darting around like a hawk on alert.

We reach the fence, ducking down beside him. Up close, he looks even younger—maybe fourteen, fifteen tops. His face is pale, and fear is etched across it. He's clutching a kitchen knife, the blade trembling slightly as he grips it tight.

"What are you doing out here?" Amanda whispers, her eyes darting around like she's expecting something to jump out at us any second.

"Shh!" The kid hushes her again, glancing toward the house we'd been watching. "They're in there," he says, his voice barely audible. "My sisters… and my mum. They're inside."

My chest tightens. The blood trail, the footprints—it all clicks together. I glance at Amanda, and I can see it in her eyes too. She understands. There's no way to sugarcoat it. Whatever's inside that house, it's not going to be good.

"Are they...?" I start to ask, but the words catch in my throat. I don't even know how to finish the question.

The boy looks at me, his eyes wide and wet, and he shakes his head. "They're not dead. But they're sick. I didn't know what to do, I just… I hid." He looks away, his face twisting in shame.

Amanda's gaze softens, her eyes lingering on the boy for a moment before she looks at me. She doesn't need to say anything—I can see it on her face. We can't just leave him here.

"What's your name?" I ask the boy, trying to keep my voice calm.

"Oliver," he whispers.

"Okay, Oliver, is that your dad in the garden?" I ask.

He nods, fresh tears welling up in his eyes.

"And was it your mum and sisters that did that to him?" I ask, catching the sharp glare Amanda throws my way.

Oliver hesitates, his lip trembling, before nodding, tears spilling down his face.

Amanda looks at me, her expression grim. I can see her trying to figure out how we should handle this. She leans closer, her voice barely audible. "We need to get him away from here. There's nothing we can do for his family. It's too dangerous to go inside."

I nod, the weight of it all pressing down on me. This isn't what I wanted. I don't want to take on the responsibility of a kid, but what other choice do we have?

"Listen, Oliver," I say, keeping my voice low and calm. "Your mum and sisters are going to be okay in the house. I'll close the gate so they can't get out, and we'll try to find some help, yeah?"

"No," Oliver says quickly, his voice trembling. "Close the patio door. Clara can climb over the fence, she does it all the time." His eyes bore into mine, pleading.

I peak around the fence to look at the open patio door, then back to the gate. The idea of even walking up to close the gate makes my stomach churn. I only said it to try to reassure the kid. But closing the patio door... that's a different level entirely. I feel the knot in my gut tighten.

Amanda lowers her bag to the ground. "I'll do it."

I frown, more out of instinct than anything else. "No, I'll do it, Amanda. He asked me, so I'll see it through. If it'll make you feel better, Oliver."

He nods, sniffling. *Great.*

I hand my bag to Amanda, hoisting my bat into both hands, giving it a few practice swings to feel its weight like I'm unfamiliar with it. It's just nerves—I need to do this, and I need to do it fast.

"Let's get this done," I mutter under my breath, trying to steel myself for what comes next.

Chapter 5

Stepping into the garden made my back stiffen, my muscles locking with each cautious step. My stomach is painfully tight, making it hard to stand up straight. My mind reels, racing through the past, trying to piece together how all those scattered moments had led me here—stepping into some random garden, knowing full well there are zombies nearby, just to close a bloody patio door to make a kid feel better. What are you playing at, Jack? I only set off to get to my parents.

I let out a sigh, glancing up at the greying clouds. "Here goes nothing..."

I approach the body of Oliver's dad, the full extent of his injuries laid bare. I feel… nothing. Looking at the inside of this man's ribcage doesn't stir the horror I would have expected. Maybe my mind just doesn't know how to process it. Humans aren't supposed to see such a thing, I suppose. Or maybe I'm getting used to this nonsense? No, I very much doubt that, sadly.

The smell is overwhelming. The air is thick with a metallic tang, mingled with the unmistakable stench of shit. Occasionally, the breeze offers a fleeting moment of relief, but it's not enough. The scent is hitting me harder than I'd like—my stomach's churning, and my mouth's starting to water in that horrible way it does before you're about to heave.

I can deal with a lot of bad smells, but poop has always been my downfall. I have distinct memories of family pets doing their business where they shouldn't—finding their lovely brown gifts and promptly doubling over, adding to the mess myself.

The building nausea spurs me forward. Stepping over the body I find myself having to make a conscious effort not to look down at the small, bloody footprints leading in the same direction I'm heading. The patio door is only a couple more metres but it's as if there's a force field preventing me from reaching it. Some unseen force begging me to yield, to turn and go back. Similar to the feeling I had about the sea of abandoned cars on the motorway. The feeling didn't do much good for me then so I'll ignore it this time.

I need to do this for Oliver and not only that, for Amanda. I want to prove I'm not a useless coward—that I can actually do the hard stuff, that I'll have her back when it counts.

I take another step, feeling the crunch of gravel beneath my boot, the sound too loud in the suffocating quiet. Just a few more feet, Jack. Keep moving. My eyes flick up to the patio doors, their glass smeared with grime and something darker. The bloody footprints trail into the house, leading me to whatever horror lies just beyond that threshold.

The house is unnaturally dark, concealing potential threats. It's difficult to tell if reaching for the handle is safe. I mean, clearly, it's not but I don't like not being able to see in there.

I reach the door, my heart hammering in my chest. I hesitate for a second, glancing back at the fence where Amanda and Oliver are hidden. Amanda's face is barely visible, her eyes fixed on me. I can't see her expression clearly, but I imagine her jaw clenched, her eyes fierce. She's counting on me. They both are. Counting on me to close this door—a pointless task in the grand scheme of things—is a bit dramatic but the thought helps.

I swallow hard, turning my attention back to the patio door. Slowly, I reach out, my hand trembling slightly as I grip the edge of the door. It's cold under my touch, and I can feel the grime sticking to my skin. I pull the door, closing it with agonising slowness, trying to make as little noise as possible. It groans in protest, and I freeze solid. I listen, every muscle tensed, waiting for something—anything—to move inside the house.

Nothing.

I release a shaky breath, having only just realised I had been holding my breath the entire time. I feel my body loosen slightly as the door clicks shut. Thank God. Now to get the bloody hell out of this garden.

I turn, taking slow steps, retracing my way in, my eyes darting to every corner, every shadow. I can almost feel eyes on me, my mind playing constant tricks on me. Every creak of the gate, every rustle of the leaves makes my skin prickle. My mind is on overdrive, conjuring phantom children with hollow eyes, creeping out from the house, reaching for me with bloody fingers.

The thoughts send shivers up my spine, and dread bites at my heels, urging me to break into a run. Funnily enough, it reminds me of when I used to turn the lights off downstairs as a kid, then bolt up the stairs in a desperate bid to escape the imaginary demon in the darkness.

A smile breaks across my face, and it feels incredible. The amusing memory of childhood silliness relieves some of the tension, and I make it back to the gate, slipping through and closing it behind me.

I see Amanda and Oliver crouching by the fence of the next house, both staring at me. "You almost look relieved, Amanda," I jest.

"Why wouldn't I be?" she retorts, a hint of sarcasm in her voice.

"Hmm, fair point," I nod.

"Did you do it?" Oliver asks, his eyes wide with hope. "Did you close the door?"

"Yes, I did, mate. They'll be fine, okay?" I say, trying to reassure him. "Do you have any other family nearby? Aunties, uncles, anyone like that?"

He pauses, considering my question, then finally says, "Yeah, my grandad lives a few streets away."

"Fantastic! Lead the way. We'll head there, make sure he's okay, and you can stay with him."

Oliver's face scrunches up a bit, but he doesn't protest.

"A word?" Amanda says, nodding to the side.

"One sec, mate. Stay right here," I tell Oliver before moving off with Amanda.

I step closer to her, keeping my voice low. "What's up?"

"What do we do if his grandad is… you know…" Her gaze drops for a moment.

"Dead?" I sigh, shaking my head. "I don't know. But Amanda, he can't stay with us."

"Why not? We can't just leave him." Her face takes on a serious look, eyes narrowing slightly.

"I don't want to babysit every kid we come across. It's not our responsibility. I know it's awful, but we need to focus on getting back on track. He'll just slow us down."

Amanda's eyes harden, and her voice is cold. "I didn't take you for being heartless, Jack."

Before I can respond, she turns sharply and heads back toward Oliver, leaving me standing there, slack-jawed in shock.

"Now you've really stepped in it, Jack," I mutter to myself.

I walk over to where Amanda and Oliver are waiting, picking up my backpack along the way. "Let's find somewhere to hole up. We need a break." Without waiting for a reply, I start walking along the fence line, hoping to spot a house that doesn't show any signs of the undead.

Thankfully, it doesn't take long before we come across a small bungalow at the far end of the row. It's detached and sits a bit back from the other properties, with high fences and thick hedges providing a sense of privacy—and maybe safety. Perfect, for now.

"Here will do. Stay put, I'll check it out," I say, my tone sharper than I intend. I catch it myself—stern and cold. I'm in a foul mood, and it's bleeding through. I glance back at Amanda, but she avoids my gaze, looking to Oliver instead. Fine. I head toward the back door, which is thankfully unlocked, and step inside.

I walk about two steps into the kitchen and stop. It's clean, very clean. The worktops are spotless and the air smells faintly of lavender. A wave of nostalgia hits me, mixed with a twinge of annoyance. It's a nasty smell and I don't understand why people insist on using it so much. It reminds me of my mum, who uses it in just about everything. Car fresheners, cleaning, washing, everything.

Suddenly, my mind flashes back to the dream I had—the one that started off so mundane, so normal, only to twist into a nightmare. I shake my head, trying to shove the memory away, and refocus on the task at hand.

Kitchen is clear so I move onto the short hall. It extends forward to the front door; a doorway looms to my right and the stairs up to the left.

I move to the right and head through the doorway that leads into the living room. It's a long room, reaching out from the very back of the house all the way to the front. Like the kitchen, this room is also spotless. The thick, soft carpet is like brand new, not a speck of dust or debris in sight.

The shelves are clean, no signs of life or struggle. And again, there's that faint lavender scent hanging in the air. I spot the plug-in air freshener in the corner and roll my eyes slightly, the image of my mum's melting face flashing into my mind; a memory of my nightmare. Satisfied the room is clear, I cross the living room and unplug the thing, tucking it away on the shelf before moving on.

I move out into the hall and reach the bottom of the stairs. I stand there for a moment staring up to the upper floor listening for movement. I've not exactly been quiet as I've stomped around in my boots. Then a pang of guilt shoots across my mind. I turn and look down at the trail of muddy, wet footprints traipsing across the laminated hall flooring. I can just about see one boot print on the nice carpet going into the living room too.

I clench my fist around the handle of the bat, my knuckles turning white. Why am I incapable of thinking before I act or speak? Looking at the nicely kept carpet on the stairs I consider removing my boots. *Too late.*

I tap the bat on the hand rail, sending a series of hollow knocks echoing up the stairwell. I wait, my breathing shallow and quiet in an effort to aid my hearing. Not a peep.

Satisfied, I begin my ascent up the stairs. Several of the floorboards creak under my weight, making me cringe—not that it matters much after I've already banged the handrail.

At the top I see three doors, all closed. It doesn't take me long to check the closest of the three. One was a bathroom, small and immaculate and the other was a bedroom, also pristine.

Moving to the third door I employ the same tactic I'd used on the others. I knock the bat on the door gently and hold my ear to the door. The entire bungalow remains silent. I reach for the handle and open the door slowly.

Immediately a smell hits me in the face but this time it's not lavender. It's the unmistakable smell of death. Arguably a nicer smell than lavender Instinctively, I cover my nose and mouth with one hand, the cricket bat ready in the other. Using the bat, I push the door open fully, revealing the source of the smell. An elderly lady lies in the bed, the sheets stained and tainted by decay.

I clench my eyes shut. This is not from any recent events—she's been gone for a long time.

The scene before me hits me hard and a deep sadness wells up from within me suddenly. Before I can even process what I am feeling, tears begin falling down my face. Something about this has unleashed the pent-up sadness within me. The face she'd died long before any of this madness. No one had found her, no one came to check up on her. The thought of this old lady, being lonely enough in life to have no one come check in on her after death hits me in the chest harder than anything I have seen so far.

What the hell is wrong with us? How did not a single person notice? Her neighbours? Her family?

I'm not sure how many minutes pass but eventually I hear movement downstairs. "Jack? Everything okay?"

Amanda. She's come in to check on me. The irony only serves to deepen the misery of this room.

I wipe away the tears and sniffle quietly. "Yeah, all good. It's clear."

I stand up, taking one last look at the woman and exit onto the landing, closing the door behind me. Downstairs I find Amanda and Oliver in the living room. Oliver is resting on the sofa and Amanda is seemingly checking through the contents on the shelves. She turns to me briefly and I catch a look of concern. I really wish she'd stop concerning herself over me. I'm not some useless puppy that needs to be coddled and looked after constantly.

I need some food, I'm starving. Hopefully that'll cheer me up.

Chapter 6

The sun is dipping low in the sky, casting long shadows over the small bungalow. We've been laying low here for most of the day, trying to rest, trying to stay out of sight. Oliver's been quiet, barely saying a word to me, and only speaking to Amanda in hushed tones. I can't blame him; the kid's been through hell. Amanda and I haven't spoken much either, just the occasional glance exchanged between us. There's not much to say anyway.

We decide to stay the night. The house is on the edge of the village, with open fields behind it that offer a relatively easy escape if things go south. It feels as safe as anywhere else in this mess, but I can't shake the feeling of unease—the knowledge that there are undead children just up the street. It gnaws at the back of my mind, refusing to let me relax. I can't help but think about how badly it must be playing on poor Oliver's mind too.

After a quick meal—shared rations, nothing fancy—we settle in for the night. The house is quiet, the kind of quiet that makes your ears ring, either that or I have tinnitus. Amanda sits near the window, her katana resting across her lap, her eyes scanning the darkening street outside. I'm on the other side of the room, leaning against the wall, my bat beside me. Oliver is curled up on the sofa, his eyes half-closed, but I can tell he's not really sleeping.

The hours pass slowly, the light outside fading until the world is painted in shades of grey and black. I try to sleep, but it's impossible. Every creak of the house settling, every rustle of wind against the windows keeps me on edge. I close my eyes, but the images of the day—the bloody footprints, the old woman in the bed—play on a loop behind my eyelids. I open them again, staring at the ceiling, trying to focus on the sound of my own breathing.

Amanda shifts slightly, her eyes meeting mine in the dim light. She doesn't say anything, just gives me a small smile. I smile back, and for a moment, there's a sense of ease between us—an unspoken release in the tension that has built up. I turn away, concealing a smile.

I decide to allow my mind to wander on a long leash. Growing up I was always told to 'let the feelings in' by my mum. She was always good at saying the right things and understanding exactly what it was that bothered me.

I think of the old lady upstairs again, imagining her final moments, rattling around this old bungalow by herself. The thought makes me sad even though I'm well aware she was more than likely fine with her circumstances. Afterall, the house is absolutely spotless and the cupboards are—amazingly for us—fully stocked. She probably went in her sleep. Best way to go, especially now.

My mind then wanders to the woodland just off the motorway. To the feeling I had that pushed us into it. It was an odd feeling, one that I can't quite remember to the fullest, nor if I've ever experienced it before.

The best way I can describe it would be to say it was like someone else's thoughts injected into my mind. A feeling of dread or… no, caution. It was a warning. A warning from God only knows where. Whatever, it wasn't a very good one.

Holy shit.

They ambushed us. They waited in the dark, just out of sight for us to come closer. The one shambling around in the opening was, what? Bait? The thought alone sends an ice knife through my core.

First there was that one that dodged me, then the bugger that opened the door, now they're setting traps. I do not like this. Not a single bit. Zombies are one thing but smart zombies? No thanks.

At least they don't sprint. I think I'd check out if they were the fast kind, they're fast enough as is.

I shake my head slightly, tugging at the leash on my mind, urging it to go in another direction. Thankfully it obliges and I think about Amanda.

Across the room, in the dim light, I can just about make out her face—her soft features seeming sharper now. The truth is, I don't really know anything about her. I know she lost her sister. I know she's from London, and I know most of her family lives in Japan. But that's about it.

I think back to our first conversations and realise she seems different now—colder, more withdrawn. Maybe it's because of me, or maybe it's just the shitty situation we're in. Either way, I must be a pretty crappy travelling companion.

I look at her, and every fibre of my being wants to go over there and talk to her. But my damn mind won't let me. The fear of upsetting her or making things awkward is too great. One fact sings loudest in my mind; she is beautiful. Seeing her in action, swinging that sword, leaves me in awe.

The last time I felt like this was… wow. When I met Sarah. My brow furrows. I can't afford distractions. I need to get to my parents.

She turns to look at me, catching me staring. I exaggeratedly clear my throat, throwing my gaze elsewhere in the room. I catch a glimpse of Oliver smirking at me, his eyes still half-open—the little shit.

"Jack?" I hear Amanda call from her side of the room.

"Uh, yeah? What's up? Something in the street?" I ask, jumping straight to business to dodge any awkwardness.

"No, nothing like that. Would you come over here?"

Her eyes are soft, and in the dim light of the candles scattered around the room, I can see her vulnerability. "Yeah, of course."

I walk over to her. "Hey."

"Hey… listen, Jack. I'm sorry about earlier."

"What do you mean? You don't—"

"Jack," she interrupts, her voice shaky. "I'm sorry. I didn't mean to call you heartless. I know you're not; you risked yourself to save me." She looks away, her eyes avoiding mine, and I notice tears forming at the corners.

There's a short silence between us before I finally speak. "You know, it's funny. I was just thinking about you—about us." I pause, watching her expression soften. "I barely know you, and yet we've spent more time together than strangers usually do." I hold her gaze as she looks up at me. "So don't be sorry. I've been so caught up in trying to make progress, I haven't taken a moment to appreciate having you on this journey with me. I wouldn't want to do this alone, so… thank you for being here."

She smiles softly at me, and I feel warmth spread through my chest. "We'll find his grandad tomorrow, then we can get back to it," she says, nodding toward Oliver, who is now truly asleep.

She places her hand on mine—it's warm, soft, and sends a pulse of electricity through my entire body. I pause, unsure of what to do next.

"I'm glad I'm here with you, Jack. And I never really thanked you, so... thank you."

I nervously rub my thumb across her fingers, regretting the gesture the moment I do it. To my surprise, she doesn't pull her hand away. Instead, she smiles at me again, her eyes soft.

"Get some rest," I say, slowly withdrawing my hand and standing up.

Amanda nods, then turns to close the curtain fully. She walks over to the large armchair, setting her things down on the small side table before curling up into a ball. She takes one last look at me in the growing darkness, her eyes lingering for a moment, before closing them.

I retreat to my original spot and sit cross-legged on the floor, the cricket bat resting across my lap. I decide to tighten that leash on my thoughts, knowing full well my mind will go haywire if I let it run loose.

I'm happy. I almost feel guilty for it, considering the state of the world. There's untold suffering out there, but here, in this small bungalow in some random village whose name I don't even know, I am happy.

I can already feel my thoughts clashing, wrestling with each other. *She doesn't like me; she's just being kind. She was just thanking me for saving her life. But… she allowed my weird thumb gesture. Maybe she was just being polite?*

For God's sake. *Sod this.* I need sleep.

Chapter 7

You rest, drifting silently through the cold expanse of the void. The blue planet below spins slowly, oblivious to your watchful gaze. You have seen galaxies collapse, stars explode and entire civilisations vanish without a trace—and yet, in just four of their 'days', this small world has amused you, for now at least. The chaos you set into motion has grown beyond your initial intentions, becoming something both familiar and unpredictable. The sheer fragility of it all is delightful.

Yet, you are dissatisfied. The chaos, as glorious as it is, lacks variety. These humans perish far too easily. Many of them fight, yes, but they fall with a predictability that makes the spectacle tedious. They break as easily as insects beneath your gaze, scattering, panicking, giving in to fear. You desire more—a challenge, a struggle worth watching. The best entertainments are the ones where the ending is uncertain.

Those who can withstand your influence are reaping a bloody harvest across the planet. Inflicting pain and suffering onto others to satisfy the itch they now have. Some are even doing it in your name, though they do not know it.

Yet you remain dissatisfied. The mindless hordes below, the ones who died and rose again. They are the unintended consequence of your influence, and while they were amusing for a time, they have become predictable. They move without thought, without purpose beyond hunger. There is no challenge in them, no spark. They lack the one thing that made humanity so interesting—their minds.

You grow bored with their ceaseless, repetitive stumbling, their endless hunger. They are too simple, too primitive. You crave something more—something new. An experiment, perhaps. You reach out once more, your will brushing against the empty minds of the dead, and you push. You push thoughts into them, commands, desires beyond hunger. You try to give them purpose, a glimmer of what they once were.

Most of them simply lack the capability to accept such higher purpose, continuing their aimless meandering in search of their next victim. But a few—a special few—respond. They do not ignore. They do not meander. They take the spark you give them and hold it, their hollow eyes flickering with something more. They are not alive, not truly, but they are more than they were. They are aware, and they understand in a limited capacity. A good starting place.

You watch them, intrigued. It turns out some of them have already retained this gift from death. That would explain those fleeting moments of amusement they have given you thus far. These few, these anomalies, they may yet prove to be entertaining. They will be your agents, your eyes and ears among the dead. They will think, they will plan, they will hunt. And perhaps, they will succeed where the others have failed. Perhaps they will find the survivors, the ones who continue to defy you, and they will bring you the chaos you crave.

You feel a ripple of excitement at the thought. This is new. This is different. It is no longer just a plague—it is a game. A game of cat and mouse, of hunter and hunted. And you, the unseen hand, will guide it all.

For a moment, you feel a ripple of something—not joy, not satisfaction, but something close. It's a fleeting thing, and you push it aside. You must remain careful; you cannot afford to draw attention. He must not sense you—not yet. Your joy, your excitement, it must be tempered, kept within. If the other were to find you, he would ruin everything. He would strip away your fun, destroy what you have built. Bring his order and its relentless tedium.

You withdraw your tendrils, retracting your awareness just enough to continue observing without interfering—without leaving a trace. You have set things into motion, and now you watch as the pieces move. The humans fight for their lives, for their loved ones, for reasons that seem almost laughable in their smallness—but they fight nonetheless. And that is what makes them worth watching.

They struggle. They fall. They rise again. And for now, that is enough.

Chapter 8

I wake to silence. The kind of silence that feels heavy, pressing in on me, making me hyper aware of every breath I take, every slight rustle of fabric as I shift. The air in the bungalow feels thick, and the dim light filtering through the curtains tells me dawn is still some time away.

Amanda is still curled up in the armchair, her chest rising and falling steadily. Across the room, Oliver is on the sofa, his back turned towards me, the blanket pulled up around his shoulders. For a moment, I just sit there, watching the stillness, trying to shake the lingering fog of sleep from my mind. Something feels off—a sensation gnawing at the edge of my awareness.

I get to my feet, moving as quietly as I can, careful not to wake Amanda. I step over to the sofa, my heart inexplicably picking up its pace, a prickling unease crawling over my skin. Oliver lies so still, too still. A knot tightens in my stomach as I reach down, my fingers trembling slightly as they grip his shoulder.

"Oliver?" I whisper, my voice barely audible.

I give his shoulder a gentle shake, rolling him over. The blanket slips away, and my breath hitches in my throat as his face comes into view. His eyes are open, black as voids, staring up at me—dead, empty. He moves faster than I can react, his mouth snapping open, teeth bared, lunging towards me with a guttural snarl.

His cold, undead hands latch onto my arm, and I feel the crushing pressure of his grip.

Panic surges through me, and I stumble backwards, my legs giving out as I hit the floor, my heart hammering wildly. The world tilts, everything spinning out of control as I struggle to push him away. His teeth snap inches from my face, the darkness of his eyes consuming my vision—

I jerk awake with a strangled gasp, my body drenched in sweat, my heart thumping painfully in my chest. The world around me is different—still dark, but the silence is real this time, heavy and oppressive. My hands are clenched around the fabric of my blanket, my knuckles white. I blink rapidly, trying to orient myself, my eyes darting around the room.

Amanda is still asleep, curled up in the armchair. Across the room, Oliver lies on the sofa, his back to me, the blanket pulled up around his shoulders. Exactly as before. I swallow hard, my throat dry, and force myself to take a deep breath.

Just a dream. Another damn dream. Getting real sick of them.

I wipe the sweat from my forehead, my body trembling as I push myself upright, my eyes never leaving Oliver. The knot in my stomach refuses to loosen, the lingering sense of dread clinging to me like a second skin. It felt so real. Too real. A warning, perhaps, like the one on the motorway. Or maybe it's just the stress of everything, the constant fear, twisting my mind into knots. I don't know.

I let out a slow, shaky breath, forcing myself to move, to stand up. I walk over to the window, glancing out into the dark street beyond. Everything is still, the world outside shrouded in shadows. I can't shake the feeling that we're running out of time—that something is coming, something I can't quite see yet. And all I can do is wait.

I look at Oliver on the sofa and then back to the bat leaning against the wall by my side. Dark thoughts swirl in my mind, but I can't afford to take any chances—not anymore. I clench my fingers around the bat tightly, its weight giving me a sense of false comfort, and walk toward Oliver.

"Jack?" Amanda's voice comes from the armchair, still heavy with sleep.

"Just a sec," I say, my eyes locked on the kid, my heart beating unevenly in my ears.

I get within arm's reach of Oliver and nudge him with the bat. His shoulder gives no resistance, moving with the jabs, limp and lifeless. My throat tightens, and I swallow the lump rising there.

"Oliver, mate, wake up." My voice trembles, and I hate the way it sounds—scared, uncertain.

I look up to the ceiling, as if searching for courage, feeling hope slowly drain from me. The silence stretches on, each second heavier than the last. I reach down, placing my hand on his shoulder, my fingers trembling as I pull him over.

His head lolls to the side, revealing his pale face. His eyes are closed, his expression peaceful—he looks as if he's simply still asleep.

Jack, what are you doing?" Amanda asks, her voice sharper now, the sleepiness fading as she takes in the scene.

I turn slightly, starting to speak, "Sorry, just a bad dream is—"

Before I can finish, Oliver crashes into my side, a blur of movement that sends us both sprawling onto the plush carpet. His guttural snarls fill the room, and a chill runs through me, rooting me to the spot, my mind going blank with shock. His teeth snap inches from my face, and panic claws at my insides. I just barely manage to jam the bat under his chin, using it to keep his gnashing jaws from sinking into me.

I am locked in a desperate struggle for survival beneath the undead fifteen-year-old. His strength is shocking—equal to, if not greater than, the woman from the other night at Amanda's sister's house. For such a small frame he's making me sweat here.

A cry for help rises in my throat, desperate to escape, but I refuse to let it out. Calling for help to deal with a small, thin child would be humiliating. Then again, I'm literally fighting for my life here. I risk a glance away from Oliver's black, frenzied eyes and gnashing teeth, looking over at Amanda. She's frozen, her eyes wide, her face stricken with horror. The realisation hits me. Now she understands. Now, I'm on my own.

Oliver's hands paw at me with limp, heavy blows—strong but without precision or coordination. It's like he's forgotten how to use them. I jerk my head side to side, barely dodging his strikes.

Think, Jack, think!

I need a way out, something to turn the tide, to gain the upper hand. The adrenaline courses through me now in full force—an electric flood tightening my muscles and heightening my senses. My heart pounds in my chest like a war drum, and my vision sharpens, narrowing my focus until the world outside fades into the background. This is it. Fight and survive.

With newfound strength, I surge the bat forward, roaring as I force it upward. I get just enough space to bring my knees up, then kick out with both feet, driving them hard into Oliver's chest. He flies backward, flailing across the room.

He crashes into the media unit, the television shattering behind him. A snarl rips from his throat—a sound that seems to vibrate in my bones. He's angry now.

I scramble to my feet, gripping the bat, ready for a hard, fast swing. Just wait for his head to come into range—step by step, Jack. Keep it simple, stay focused. Step one, step two...

Oliver stands up—and just stands there. He bares his teeth repeatedly, his void-like eyes locked on me, studying.

What the fuck?

The display is sickening, and I feel the effects of the adrenaline spike begin to fade, leaving me shaky. He cocks his head to one side like a dog trying to understand something.

My fingers fidget on the handle of the bat, my palms beginning to sweat. The nervousness creeps back in, trailed by that same cold dread I've experienced so many times.

I let out a war cry—choked by my frayed nerves—and rush forward, swinging the bat with all my strength. In my desperation to end this, I choose power over precision.

As I close the distance, the bat swings in a wide arc towards Oliver. Too high. The bat fails to connect with anything as it sails through empty air, slipping from my hands—the rubberised grip now slick with sweat.

The bat slams into the wall, and my hands complete their swing—carried by momentum—leaving me wide open. Oliver reacts like a hair-trigger, slamming into me with a force that instantly drives the air from my lungs.

One of his hands slams into my throat, making me choke violently. The force of his tackle sends us hurtling backward, my back slamming into the wall. The impact stuns me, and for a moment, I'm dazed—almost enough time for him to tear a chunk of my flesh out.

I scramble, disoriented, my arms flailing and punching wildly at my attacker—then suddenly, he stops. Unable to stop myself in time, I shove him away and dart to the side, distancing myself.

As my senses return, I see Amanda standing over Oliver, her katana slick with blood, his head rolling a few feet away. Her eyes are filled with tears, her face impassive as she stands frozen, staring straight ahead.

I am at a complete loss for words. Amanda's entire body trembles as she stands there, her gaze empty. Nausea rises within me, but I force it down.

"Amanda, thank you—"

"Don't," she cuts me off.

I watch as she straightens, her katana slipping from her grasp and landing with a dull thud on the carpet. Her face remains blank, her only visible emotion being the tears streaming silently down her cheeks.

Without another word, she walks over to the armchair and curls into a tight ball, her back to me. She makes no sound, but I can see her body subtly bobbing up and down. She's sobbing.

I rub my eyes, the exhaustion of the fight settling deep into my bones. I look down at Oliver, my mind racing with questions. How did he turn? He must have been bitten, but he never once complained about pain or showed any signs.

I crouch beside him, glancing up to ensure Amanda isn't watching. I roll up his sleeves—nothing. Not a scratch. I move to his legs, rolling up each trouser leg. The right one is clear, no injuries. But the left leg... there's a nasty bite on his ankle. The bite is small, and images of those small bloody footprints flash through my mind.

It's mad to think we will live in a world where your family members might tear you apart one day. I hope my parents are okay. I hope they don't tear me apart when I find them.

Leaving Amanda to herself, I pick Oliver up and hold him in my arms. For how strong he was, he isn't heavy at all. The fact it took all my strength to knock him away amazes me.

I carry him to the backdoor and open it. The cold early morning air slams me in the face sending a chill throughout my body.

"Soon we'll have dead people *and* the cold to contend with." I mumble to myself under my breath.

I place Oliver down near some bushes in the garden, pausing to look around. The sky is clear, making it seem even colder, but it's the stars that catch my attention. I'm so used to not seeing them because of the clouds and light pollution, but tonight they shine so brightly—as if in defiance of the evil happening down here.

The stars have always amazed me, even as a child. It blew my mind to learn I was essentially looking into the past. Some of the stars up there, clearly visible now, no longer exist—yet their light lives on. Their brilliant legacy.

My eyes wander across the field of stars, finally settling on a particularly bright, yellow one. The sight of it sends a pang of short-lived nausea through my stomach. The shade of yellow—it's not like the others. It's wrong.

A memory claws its way into my thoughts. A dream. I had it the night everything went to hell—a dream of a sickly yellow eye looking down on us. The star reminds me of that eye.

"Hmm," I chuckle to myself. I must just have an overactive imagination.

I shake my head and turn, walking back into the bungalow kitchen. I lock the backdoor, testing the handle with a few quick tugs to ensure the lock is truly engaged.

The kitchen remains unspoiled. There are some open packets of crisps on the worktop—no doubt Oliver's doing—but other than that, it's as clean as when I first found it.

My stomach rumbles, and I decide that sleep is out of the question; I might as well get something to eat. I flick the kettle on and open the cupboard doors over the work surface.

Inside is a cornucopia of canned goods—vegetables, beans, soups, mystery meats, even a couple of those canned pies. On the other side are several jars. One filled with cookies, another with sweets, some with cereals. A genuine elderly kitchen.

I grab the jar of sweets and close the cupboards. The kettle boils and flicks itself off with that click every British person worth their salt knows by heart.

I put a single teaspoon of sugar in a mug, followed by a teabag. What the hell—may as well treat myself. I add an adventurous second spoonful of sugar.

I settle onto a smaller armchair opposite Amanda, who is sleeping fitfully, and sip my tea, eating toffees and other assorted sweets.

I allow myself to sink into this little moment. A slice of that fleeting normalcy I so desperately miss. I need to enjoy the smaller things more often; life is miserable enough without them.

Chapter 9

The light seems harsh this morning. According to the clock on the wall it is ten-past-ten. A later start than I'd have liked but I think we all… both, need our rest.

I look down to the blanket of empty sweet wrappers that covers me. "Hmm, I need to brush my teeth."

I glance over to the armchair where Amanda had been sleeping, only to find it empty. Her blanket is neatly folded and placed on the armrest.

"Amanda?" I call out, my voice just loud enough to carry through the nearest rooms.

No response.

I frown, trying not to let worry take hold. I stand, dusting myself off and bending to pick up the stray wrappers, scrunching them all into a ball in my hand. I don't even remember falling asleep. I ate sweets—evidently—and drank a cup of tea. That's it. I must have dozed off.

I walk into the kitchen, placing the mug by the sink and tossing the ball of wrappers into the bin. I stop and listen for a moment, hoping to hear some movement elsewhere in the bungalow. Still nothing. A small knot of concern starts to form, but I push it aside.

Then my heart sinks. The kettle won't turn on. I push the switch down, but nothing happens. "God, no. Please no."

I turn to the fridge, swinging the door open. The little light inside stays dark.

I close my eyes in defeat. "Of course," I whisper. I knew it was going to happen. If I'm honest with myself, I'm surprised it took this long. The power always goes out eventually.

I don't claim to know much about power station maintenance, especially nuclear power—which is all we have in Britain now—but surely, it can't be too difficult. There must be fail-safes, and most of it is automated, right? But that doesn't matter now.

I turn quickly to look at the stove. Gas. Maybe there's still gas left in the pipes. I don't even know if gas runs without electricity. Shit, there's so much I don't know.

I make an effort to refocus my mind, to pull it back from the storm of thoughts and concerns. One thing at a time. I turn the gas hob on, the little igniter clicking a few times before a beautiful little blue flame appears. I twist the knob, enlarging the flames watching as they turn orange.

I can still have a cup of tea.

I make two cups and as I pour the milk into the second—Amanda's cup—I begin to actually worry. I've not heard a peep from in the bungalow.

Did I see her things? Her sword?

I rush back into the room and my gut flips, making me feel nauseous; her sword is missing leaving only the faint crimson outline on the once pristine carpet.

I stare at the empty space, the bloody outline, my stomach twisting, threatening to expel what little remains inside it. A hollow feeling spreads through my chest as panic begins to build, gnawing at the edges of my mind. My first instinct is to run outside, to call her name, to find her. But I clench my teeth, squeezing my eyes shut. No, think, Jack. Running around blindly won't help.

She's smart—smarter than I am. She wouldn't just leave without a reason. Not without telling me, at least. Well, I'd like to think so anyway. I force myself to breathe, to slow the rapid beat of my heart. She's out there, and she's got a plan, she has to have a plan. I have to trust her, like she's trusted me on multiple occasions.

"Okay, Jack, focus," I mutter, trying to keep my voice steady. I glance at the two mugs of tea on the counter, both steaming faintly. The absurdity of it strikes me—tea, like it's just another normal morning. I need to be practical. But then again, I did tell myself to enjoy the normal things, the little things. I'm finding myself at odds with my own thoughts more and more. *Focus.*

I grab the tea meant for Amanda, taking a long sip from my own cup. The warmth settles something within me, giving me a moment to collect my thoughts. I need to be ready for when she comes back. I need to trust that she will come back.

I take a deep breath and start moving. First things first—I gather what I can, checking over our supplies. I organise everything: water, canned food, whatever essentials we have left. My hands move automatically, keeping me focused, keeping the fear at bay. I stop by the window and look out at the quiet street. There's nothing out there, not yet, at least.

I hope she's being careful. I really do. But if anything's gone wrong, I need to be ready to act. I clench my fists reflexively and without thought. I look at my hands taking note of the worry I feel bubbling away inside me.

She's coming back, I tell myself, repeating the words like a mantra. She's coming back.
I pace around the bungalow, the silence gnawing at me. Amanda's tea sits untouched, long since gone cold, and I feel a growing restlessness—maybe even nervousness. I can't decide which. Probably both.

She's been gone for hours now, and I can tell by the fading light that it will be getting dark soon, that and the clock on the wall. The thought of heading out there to look for her crosses my mind again, but I know it's a terrible idea. Stumbling through the village in the dark isn't exactly an appealing prospect, especially now that the power's out and there will be no street lights to guide me.

I glance at a picture of a cat on the mantelpiece, a silly thought escaping my lips, "Cat's eyes would be great right about now."

I complete another round of window peeking, a habit I've developed over the last few hours to keep my body moving, my mind from spiralling. But there's still no sign of Amanda. Nothing and no one. The village feels too quiet—dead, if I'm being honest.

I sit back down, the silence creeping in again. The only sound in the room is the ticking of the old clock, counting down the seconds, each one seeming to echo in the quiet space. I find myself staring at the door, half-expecting it to open at any moment, for Amanda to walk back in and shake her head at me for worrying.

Minutes pass, and nothing happens. I catch myself drumming my fingers on the armrest, my eyes still on the door. "You better be alright, Amanda," I mumble, more to myself than to anyone else. "Come back soon, alright? I don't want to do this alone…"

Finally, the sun dips beneath the horizon, the dim light in the room fading into near darkness. I take a deep breath, feeling my nerves spike. This isn't just restlessness anymore—it's fear. I hate it. My instincts scream at me to get out there, to do something, but my brain is quick to remind me what happened the last time I acted on impulse. Oliver. His dark eyes, the horrible snarl, and Amanda standing over him, her sword dripping in blood. Ignoring the clear warnings of my dream. Sadly, just one of many impulsive decisions I've made that ended less than ideally.

I can't let fear drive me. Amanda is tough. She'll find her way back.

I force myself to stand, walking back to the kitchen, my movements stiff. I light a few candles, their flickering light casting long shadows across the walls. I need to stay calm, stay ready. She will be back. I have to believe that.

I sink into the armchair, staring into the candle flame, the soft light giving a fragile comfort. I'll wait. And when she gets back, I'll make sure to thank her properly for what she did, for saving me. She better get back soon.

But what if she has left me? Abandoned me to continue my mission alone? I try to think rationally, but the fear of being alone weighs heavier on me than I'd have ever expected. Maybe it's because the power's out and the darkness feels different now—more oppressive, more alive. It seems to watch me, whispering all the fears I'm trying to bury, and it only compounds my loneliness. I don't know.

It's all starting to become too much—the dreams, Nick, Oliver, Amanda, my journey that I can't seem to make any damn progress on. Everything feels like it's pushing down on me, crushing me under the weight of it all.

I let out a long sigh, the sound echoing in the otherwise still room. It sets my teeth on edge. Breaking the silence feels wrong, almost dangerous. There's something about the quiet that feels safer somehow— like if I stay silent, the darkness won't notice me, won't reach out and swallow me whole.

I hate the dark.

I get up again, unable to sit still. My hand finds the bat as I pace back and forth across the room, each step sounding louder in the emptiness. My eyes flicker to the window, then back to the door. I wish I could see out there, see her coming back. But there's only darkness.

Just the void staring back at me, daring me to make a move, to go out and face it.

I need to stay rational, stay grounded, but all I can think of is how empty it all feels. The silence, the shadows, the absence of Amanda—it's eating away at me, and I'm not sure how much longer I can stand it. It's taken until now, wrapped in doubt and silence, alone in the darkness, for me to accept a horrible truth: I'm not cut out for this.

The survivors in my books all made it seem so easy. They'd charge head first into hordes of the undead with nothing but a knife or a bat and take them out in droves without so much as a scratch. Life just isn't like that. This is real, and I'm woefully unprepared.

It's the mental toll that's wearing me down more than anything else. I don't even realise how deeply it's affecting me—the death, the violence, the constant threat to my life—until it all hits me out of the blue. My mind can't repress it anymore, and I'm left feeling raw, exposed. God, this is shit. And to think, I used to wish for something like this, just because I had a moderately bad day at the office.

You're an idiot Jack.

A tapping sound tears me from my thoughts, and I tense, keeping my breaths shallow and quiet. Could it have been my mind playing tricks on me? The more I replay the sound in my head, the less likely that seems.

No. It's real. There it is again.

Three soft taps against the window. The curtains are drawn, and I can't see what's causing the noise, but my mind jumps in to fill the gaps. I picture phantom corpses and twisted faces peering through the glass, and my blood runs cold.

My overactive imagination strikes again. I wait, listening—again, three soft taps, the rhythm slightly off this time.

Suddenly, the idea of a zombie tapping on the window fills me with ice-cold dread—a violently disgusting thought that I try my hardest to push down. But it refuses to leave my mind as I rise slowly from the chair.

My eyes stay glued to the curtains as I approach. Four taps this time, followed quickly by five. The sound feels so familiar, but my mind won't let me recognize it, replacing any chance of innocence with illusory terror.

With a deep breath—the cool, still air filling my lungs doing little to add courage—I pull back the curtains, revealing the window and dispelling the imaginary undead.

A branch.

It was a bloody branch. The relief that washes over me in this exact moment is almost indescribable. I knew it sounded familiar.

"That's it. I've had it. I'm going out," I announce into the silence, my voice laced with false confidence.

I hastily collect my things, my backpack now heavier with the canned goods and supplies from the kitchen.

I open the front door and step out into the cold morning air. The wind has picked up—hence the damn branch. It feels colder than usual, with light droplets of rain starting to patter against my face. The outside world seems more uninviting than ever before.

A solitary, clear thought cuts through the chaos in my head: why leave a safe place in favour of the dark unknown?

Fair point, me.

I turn and re-enter the bungalow, deciding that the rational choice is to wait until dawn before going to look for Amanda.

Three taps later, I'm back outside, swatting at the branch to stop it from disturbing me anymore. Back in the front room, I wait patiently, listening for any further sounds. Silence. Finally.

In the quiet I've restored for myself; my mind starts its new hobby: wandering. I'm a mess. My mind feels more like an enemy than an ally lately, and it's strange how much more introspective I've become. The fact that I'm even thinking all of this just proves I need to sort my head out.

Why'd you have to leave, Amanda?

Chapter 10

I wake with a start, my fingers numb, clutching the cricket bat like a lifeline. I blink blearily, the room slowly coming into focus. The soft light of dawn spills through the small gap in the curtains, casting a faint glow over the room. I glance at the clock on the wall—a couple minutes past seven.

I let out a groan, my body stiff from having slept in an awkward position. I must have dozed off while waiting, the bat still in my grip in case something—anything—decided to come through the door or windows. For a moment, I allow myself to believe everything is okay, that Amanda is just in the next room. But the silence weighs heavily, and I know better.

She still hasn't returned.

I push myself to my feet, rubbing the sleep from my eyes, my mind snapping back to focus. Today, I have a mission—find Amanda. I'm not going to sit around again wasting another day, letting the silence and doubt eat away at me. No more hesitating. I'll find her.

I move through the small bungalow, gathering the supplies I packed last night. The weight of the backpack settles across my shoulders, a familiar and reassuring feeling. The cricket bat is once again in my hand, and I give it a test swing, letting the weight move with me, a gesture that is fast becoming more habit than of any practical use.

After a final scan of the room—Amanda's folded blanket still on the armchair—I head to the door, taking a deep breath before stepping outside.

The early morning air is cold, biting against my exposed skin. The wind has died down, and the rain has stopped, leaving a damp chill that clings to everything. The village is eerily quiet again, as if I expected anything different.

I pull the door closed behind me, listening to the faint click of the latch. No going back now. I turn and start walking, my eyes scanning the rows of small houses and gardens. There's something unsettling about the stillness—no cars, no people, not even the sound of birdsong. It's something I've noticed every day now, something I cannot get used to.

I tighten my grip on the bat, my steps slow and cautious as I move down the street. Every corner, every shadow feels like it could hold danger, and I'm hyper-aware of every rustle of leaves or creak of a distant door. The small village feels empty, yet I know better than to assume I'm alone.

The first house I pass looks like it's been abandoned—the windows are broken, the front door hanging open. I peer inside briefly, seeing nothing but darkness and dust. I move on, my eyes scanning for any signs of movement, any hint of Amanda.

A few more steps, and I reach a small corner shop. The windows are intact, but the door is slightly ajar. I pause, my breath catching in my throat as I listen. Nothing. I walk up and push the door open with the bat, the creak echoing in the quiet making me cringe. I step inside, the air as cold as outside. The shelves are mostly empty, stripped of anything useful, but I'm not here for supplies.

"Amanda?" I call softly, my voice barely more than a whisper. It feels wrong to speak out loud, as if I'm breaking some unspoken rule. I listen, straining to hear over the drumming in my chest but there's no response.

I let out a sigh, my shoulders sagging slightly. She's not here. I turn, stepping back out into the street, my eyes scanning the surrounding buildings.

I hear something, a fast rhythmic sound that is almost too quiet to hear, distant but definitely coming closer, growing in volume. In the silence it's easy to hear but I cannot quiet make out the sound nor its source.

I wait for a moment, my eyes shifting about my surroundings every few seconds to make sure I'm not snuck up on.

The sound grows and eventually it becomes clear to me, it's the sound of running. No, sprinting. The steady thrum of fast footfalls on the pavement. The slapping sound tells me whoever is doing the running is barefoot.

Barefoot running outside? I approach the corner of the shop building to look in the direction of the sound. As I approach however, more sounds catch my attention.

The barefoot runner is accompanied by another set of feet, not quite as fast.

I risk a peek around the corner and the sight before me confuses me more than anything else.

I see a portly man, dressed only in boxer shorts and a bathrobe—open and flowing behind him as he runs—he is red-faced and clearly out of steam.

My eyes move forwards to see his pursuer. A woman with wild, black eyes. She is clothed and stained almost head to toe in old brown blood.

I duck backwards behind the wall hoping I wasn't spotted. "Shit."

I hear no shouting or hollering, only the sound of feet coming ever closer. What do I do? Do I help the man? Hide? I'm trying to look for Amanda, besides the last person we helped tried to kill me. It's different now, I need to look after myself first.

The man's frantic footfalls are getting louder, closer. I grip the bat tightly, my mind racing. *Do I help him?* He's clearly in trouble, but helping could mean exposing myself to the danger I'm trying so hard to avoid. I peek around the corner once more. The man is staggering, his legs starting to give out beneath him. The woman behind him is relentless—her eyes hollow, filled only with hunger.

I clench my teeth, my chest tightening. Everything in me screams to stay hidden, to let this play out without involving myself. I can't risk it. Not now, not after everything that's happened. But watching this man, defenceless, about to be torn apart—it makes me feel sick.

Memories of Nigel flood my mind. A similar situation—one where I let my neighbour die.

The pounding gets closer, and I have to make a choice. Damn it, Jack. Think.

"Help! Somebody, help!" The man's voice cracks as he calls out, and he turns his head back, seeing the zombie closing in. His eyes are filled with sheer desperation.

I take a deep breath, and without thinking much more, I step out from behind the corner, the bat held up and ready. I can't just let him die. Not like this.

The man's gaze catches mine, and for a brief second, there's a flicker of hope in his eyes. His feet stumble, his momentum slowing, and he falls to his knees, breathless and defeated. The undead woman lunges forward, her fingers curling, ready to grab onto him.

I don't give myself time to hesitate. I rush towards her, my bat swinging wide narrowly avoiding the kneeling man's head. The impact sends a sickening crack through the air, and she staggers, her head jerking sideways. I swing again, a desperate roar escaping my lips as I connect once more, this time sending her crumpling to the ground.

The man is gasping, his face streaked with tears and sweat. He looks up at me, his eyes wide, a mix of gratitude and sheer terror.

"Come on!" I shout, reaching down to grab his arm. "Get up, get up!"

He struggles to his feet, his legs shaking, and I pull him with me, glancing behind us. The woman on the ground twitches, her limbs jerking in an unnatural way. She isn't down for good. Not yet. We have to move.

"Where—where are we going?" the man pants, struggling to keep pace as we run down the street.

"Anywhere but here!" I shout, pulling him along. We round a corner, and I lead him down a narrow alley between two houses, hoping to put some distance between us and the undead.

We reach a small garden, hidden behind a wooden fence, and I push the gate open, urging the man inside. We both collapse to the ground, gasping for breath, the adrenaline still coursing through my veins.

For a moment, there's silence—just the sound of our ragged breathing. I glance over at him, taking in the dishevelled state of his robe, the way his face contorts itself in his exhaustion. He looks at me, his eyes wide and fearful, but there's a flicker of gratitude there too.

"Thanks, mate," he whispers, his voice strained. "Honestly, thanks. I thought... I thought that was it." He lets out a forced chuckle.

I nod, trying to steady my own breathing. "Don't mention it. Just... stay quiet, okay? We don't want to draw any more of them."

"More of them? There's more?" His eyes dart around the garden, the look of concern returning to his face.

What? Was that a serious question? The look on his face tells me it was, but how is that possible? It's been what... wow, four days now. How has he not seen more?

"What do you mean?" I ask, failing to hide my surprise.

"There's more of those things? She was sick, mate. She just came to pick up Isabelle."

I frown, my confusion evident. "Isabelle? Who was sick?"

"Sorry," he pauses, taking a few deep breaths. "Isabelle's my daughter. That woman was her mother—my ex-wife. She came over to pick Izzy up but collapsed. I put her in the spare bedroom, but when she woke up, she attacked us."

"Wednesday morning?" I ask, a little lost at the level of detail this man is sharing with a stranger.

"Yeah, Wednesday. So, it's some kind of bug? More people are sick like Jo?"

"Listen, umm..."

"Kevin," he says, holding his hand out.

I take his hand and shake it. His grip is strong, and I wonder why he didn't deal with this 'Jo' himself. But who am I to judge, I suppose.

"Jack. Good to meet you. Listen, Kevin, there's no easy way to say this, so I'll just come out with it. They're dead. Or, undead, rather."

Kevin stares at me, his expression vacant. Did he even hear me? "Kevin?"

"Like... zombies?" he asks, his eyebrows shooting up.

"Erm... yeah," I say, looking down. "It's a lot to process, I know, but I've come from Wigan and seen more than enough of them."

"No, no, I believe you."

"You do?" I can't help the surprise in my voice.

"Yeah, it makes sense, doesn't it..." He trails off, turning away from me.

I'm about to say something, but then I notice his shoulders trembling, and hear the slight sniffle as he wipes at his eyes. I close my mouth, choosing instead to stay silent, letting him have this moment.

Jo—his attacker and apparent ex-wife—shuffles past on the other side of the fence we're hunkered behind, and we both fall silent and still. Kevin keeps his eyes on me the entire time.

I hold a finger to my lips, then gesture for him to follow me. I don't exactly know why, but I can't help feeling sorry for him. I don't know how he's managed to miss everything going on, why he's dressed the way he is, or even if I fully believe his story. Aside from Amanda and Nick, everyone I've met has been a deranged psychopath. Yet here I am, helping him. I feel compelled to. I'm the experienced one for once, making it kind of my duty to step up and be there for him.

It's strange, and I don't fully understand why I feel this way, but I'll keep an eye on him for now. I have the bat, and he doesn't.

I lead the way to the back door of the house, cautiously testing the handle. It turns easily, and the door opens with a soft sound, the weather-stripping parting quietly.

As I step into the kitchen, the acrid stench of ammonia hits me in the face like a punch, forcing me to jerk my head back and cover my mouth.

"What's wrong?" Kevin asks nervously from behind me.

"It stinks of cat piss," I mutter, cautiously moving further into the kitchen.

The room itself is relatively tidy—nothing alarming. Just some rubbish scattered across the counters and a few unwashed plates in the sink. Messy, but nothing out of the ordinary.

I take another step, my boots scuffing lightly against the linoleum floor. The acrid stench clings to the back of my throat, and I instinctively pull back, covering my mouth. Despite the nausea building, I force myself to push through, eyes scanning the kitchen. It's strange how normal this house feels—like the world outside hasn't collapsed into chaos. But it's still surreal. Every time I step into a house that isn't mine, it feels... wrong, like I'm trespassing in a life that's now gone.

Kevin follows behind, his breath still heavy from the sprint, his eyes darting from corner to corner. He's on edge, and who could blame him? I note the way he moves—sluggish from exhaustion. His stamina might be an issue if things go south. Another mental log to keep.

We move further into the house. It's open-plan, making it easier to see any potential dangers without barriers in the way. There are no signs of people—living or otherwise—but what I do see sets my nerves on edge. Kevin spots it too. His breathing slows, like he's consciously trying to stay as quiet as possible.

In the centre of the living room, there's a dark pool of blood. The scene tells its story clearly—something violent happened here. The blood doesn't look fresh, which is somewhat relieving, but the smeared footprints leading towards the stairs are anything but. A chill settles in my gut. I feel the bat in my hands and tighten my grip. But a thought strikes me—Kevin isn't armed. If something's waiting for us upstairs, we'll need more than just one heavy swinging object.

"Grab a weapon," I whisper, keeping my eyes on the staircase. "Whatever you can find."

Kevin doesn't say anything, just nods and starts searching. After a few minutes, he settles on a large kitchen knife, holding it awkwardly at first, then gripping it tightly. He looks at me and gives a nod—ready as he'll ever be.

I take a step towards the stairs, the floor creaking softly beneath my boot. A sound—faint, like a shuffle—comes from above, and I hold myself, my mouth going dry. I swallow, trying to gather what little courage I have left. Just as I prepare to take another step, I feel Kevin's hand on my shoulder.

"What's the point?" he whispers.

His words hit me like a bell ringing in the quiet of my mind. What is the point indeed? I look at the stairs again, my heart thudding in my ears. Jesus, I was about to risk my life—our lives—for what? Curiosity? A misguided sense of duty? I let out a slow breath, feeling the tension loosen just slightly.

"Fair point…" I murmur, glancing back at Kevin. His face is pale, but his eyes are resolute. I nod towards the front door. "We need to get you sorted first—gear, clothes, something proper. Let's try the next house."

Kevin looks down at himself, barefoot, wearing only a bathrobe, and nods, a small, grim smile tugging at his lips. Without another word, we head towards the door, leaving the ominous stairs—and whatever might be waiting above—behind us. All the while I'm constantly thinking on my main objective. Find Amanda.

Chapter 11

We've made it into a house further down the street. The front door had been forced open at some point, the lock hanging loose, the frame splintered. Kevin looks at it nervously as we step inside, and I can tell he's still adjusting to all of this, somehow. I guess we both are, but at least I've had a bit more time. I hope he'll tell me his story, more to pacify my curiosity than anything else.

The place is empty, as far as I can tell. No signs of people, no immediate signs of danger. I nod at Kevin, and we move through the hallway, our footsteps muffled on the old carpet. He's got the knife, and I keep my bat close, always ready. It feels like every corner holds a potential threat—every room we enter is like opening Pandora's box, not knowing what bat dodging, stealthy ambushing horrors await.

We searched through the ground floor first. The house has an open, yet cluttered feel to it, like it was lived in but never quite organised. A stack of magazines spills across the coffee table, a kid's toy doll lies discarded by the stairs, and there are half-full mugs of tea sitting on coasters. It's like they just left—or were taken by surprise.

"We need to find something better for you to use," I mutter, nodding towards Kevin's knife. "Something with a bit more heft."

Kevin doesn't say much, just gives a tight nod and starts rummaging through the living room, pulling open drawers and peering into cabinets. I can see his nerves—every little creak or gust of wind from outside makes him flinch, makes his hand tighten on the knife. I don't blame him. My heart's been pounding ever since we stepped in here. Funny how it feels safer outside now.

In the kitchen, I finally spot something. Leaning against the back door, partially hidden behind some old umbrellas, is a crowbar. I grab it, turning it over in my hands. It's got some heft to it, and I know it'll do the job if it needs to.

"Hey, Kevin," I call, and he comes over, his eyes wide. I hand him the crowbar, and he takes it, nodding slowly.

"This... yeah, this is good," he says, a bit of relief in his voice. He tests its weight, giving it a few swings. It's awkward, but it's better than a knife, that's for sure.

As I watch him test the crowbar, I take a moment to properly assess the man for the first time. He's large and stocky—in his mid-forties if I had to guess—with broad shoulders and a gut. His hands are rough and thick—he strikes me as someone used to manual labour. The way he handles the crowbar, the ease with which he swings it, only adds to that impression. He inspects the bar, rubbing a hand through his short, unkempt beard. Then he looks at me, giving a small, curt smile.

After we confirm the house is clear, we settle down for a bit. I find some canned soup in one of the cupboards, along with a few bottles of water. Kevin's already sitting at the kitchen table, staring off into space, his shoulders slumped.

I set the cans down in front of him, grabbing a couple of spoons from a drawer. "Here, eat something," I say, my voice softer than before. I take a seat across from him, and we eat in silence for a while—the only sound the slurping of soup.

Kevin eventually looks up, his eyes tired but curious. "How long have you been out here? You know, on your own?"

I take a sip of water, shrugging. "Feels like forever, but it's only been a few days. Four, I think. I've been moving since the start, trying to stay ahead of things. Avoiding people, mostly."

He nods, looking down at his can. "Yeah, I guess that makes sense. Safer that way."

There's a moment of silence, and I take a breath, deciding it's time to ask. "Hey, Kev... have you seen anyone else around? A woman? Dark hair, about my age? Her name's Amanda."

Kevin looks up, frowning as if thinking hard. He shakes his head slowly. "No, mate. Just Jo... and Izzy. Haven't seen anyone else. Been busy locked in my own bathroom."

I nod, trying not to let the disappointment show. I was hoping for something—anything. But there's nothing. I force a smile, shrugging like it's no big deal. "Yeah, figured. Just thought I'd ask."

Kevin's gaze lingers on me, and he clears his throat. "She someone important?"

I pause, my fingers drumming on the table. "Yeah. Yeah, she is." I don't elaborate, and Kevin doesn't push. We go back to eating, the silence settling over us once more—heavier now, but not entirely uncomfortable.

Is she someone important to me? Amanda is special, but beyond the circumstances of how we met, and the shared horrors we've faced, we barely know each other. Kevin doesn't need to know all of that.

After a while, Kevin speaks up again, his voice low. "You think it'll get better? Any of this?"

I don't have an answer for him. I wish I did. Instead, I look out the window at the empty street, the wind rustling the leaves, the shadows growing longer. "I don't know," I admit. "I think we just... have to keep moving. Keep surviving. Maybe that's all we can do."

Kevin nods, his eyes distant, and we lapse into silence again. It's a fragile sort of peace, but for now, it's enough.

A thought dawns on me: where are all the undead? I've barely seen any since arriving in the village, yet there are signs that they were here. The thought lingers in my mind as I sip cold tomato soup, careful not to cut my lip on the can.

"Think it's connected to all that nonsense in Europe?" Kevin asks, breaking my train of thought.

"Hmm? The riots?" I ask, taking a big gulp of water from my bottle. "Probably, yeah. I bet it moved through the continent before making its way here."

"So, you've seen more of them?" he asks, his mouth full.

"Yeah, a fair few. Had some close calls too."

"And they're... you know... really dead?"

I force a smile. "Yeah, sorry."

Kevin looks down, slowly shaking his head. "I'm going to see if I can grab anything to wear."

"Give me a shout if you need me, yeah?" I say as he walks towards the stairs. We checked everything earlier, so he shouldn't need my help. Unless he needs a hand getting dressed, of course. Let's hope not.

Alone, having finished my cold soup, I look around the room. Family photos hang on the wall, showing a warm, happy family. Their smiles are full of love, the kind that's so evident it leaps out of the picture. Yet, looking at them fills me with a deep sense of sadness. All I can think about is loss—what they might have endured, what they might have lost.

There's no blood in the house, so I assume the door was forced open by looters. But then, nothing seems to have been taken; we found water and canned food, after all. It doesn't make sense—none of this does. I just hope that wherever the family who lived here are, they're out there surviving.

Eventually, Kevin comes back downstairs, no doubt having ransacked wardrobes and drawers for something that fits. I stifle a smile as he rounds the corner from the stairway. He's still wearing the robe, for some reason, but underneath I can see an oversized T-shirt with an obscure band logo on it. For trousers, he's got a pair of worn joggers, complemented by a fresh-looking pair of white trainers.

"What's with the robe?" I ask, smiling.

"I dunno'. Didn't feel right leaving it behind in a stranger's house," he says, tying it off at the waist. "Reminds me of home."

"Fair enough," I reply, not wanting to tell him it could be a grab hazard. I'll let him have his comfort.

"Right then, mate—sorry, Jack," he corrects himself, sitting down beside me. "What's your plan?"

"I need to find Amanda. Then..." I trail off, not entirely sure if I should tell him about my parents or the farm.

"No plan after that, then? Why don't you come with me?" he asks, looking me directly in the eyes.

"You've got a plan already?" I raise an eyebrow.

"Yeah, I need to fetch my son from uni. He's only been there a week or so. I need to make sure he's okay."

"What university does he go to?"

"Nottingham."

What. Are. The. Odds.

"Wow, well... I'll be heading that way after I find Amanda, I think. I've got family down there myself."

A big grin spreads across his face. "Well then! That settles it." He pats my back with one of his large, rough hands. "Jack, mate, honestly—thank you. I'm glad we bumped into each other. Glad we can travel together too; I'll need someone to show me the ropes and all that."

I let out a forced smile, trying to hide my caution about the idea of travelling with him. Kevin seems great, but I don't know him from the next guy. Then again, I didn't know Amanda either. And yet, here I am—postponing my own journey to find her. Two people I've saved. Two people I've adopted. Maybe I am more like the characters in my books after all... Nah.

We collect our things and head out into the street. Quiet again with no sign of anything alive or dead.

"I don't like how quiet it is." I say, more to myself than to Kevin.

"No?"

"No." I hesitate. "There should be..." I trail off, then shake my head. "I've just realised how much I hate saying the word 'zombie' out loud."

"Ha, well let's choose a different name for them then. What about Biters?" Kevin says with a laugh.

I look at him incredulously. "Biters?"

"Yeah, why not? They bite, don't they?"

I raise my eyebrows, giving him that universal 'I suppose so' face, turning down the corners of my mouth. "Biters it is, then. But seriously, there should be more of them here."

We walk for about five minutes, Kevin leading the way towards the centre of the village. The streets are still and empty, every sound magnified in the quiet. We pass a small cluster of shops—just the usual lineup: a convenience store, a Chinese takeaway, a chippy with its familiar faded sign, and, of course, the obligatory barber shop with its spinning red, white, and blue pole. The kind of places that probably hadn't changed much since the '80s.

The air is thick with stillness, and the sight of those familiar shops feels like a relic of normality in a world that's anything but. Kevin seems focused, his eyes scanning the area, and I stay close behind, gripping my bat. It's strange to be moving through a place that would have been bustling just days ago, now reduced to an eerie snapshot of life on pause.

"I was there only a few days ago." Kevin says pointing at the barbers.

I look at his hair and wonder if he was just dropping someone off. The thought causes a chuckle to break from my lips.

"Say something?" Kevin asks, looking over his shoulder.

"No, just mumbling to myself." I reply, trying to hide my amusement.

"Hold up. Look," he says, his voice low, his arm raising to point down the street.

I step up beside him, squinting against the glare of daylight. At first, I see nothing but the empty street ahead, but then it catches my eye—a lone figure, shuffling slowly, its back turned towards us.

The figure is moving sluggishly, barely at a crawl, the gait uneven and swaying. Something about it feels wrong, familiar in a way that makes my stomach clench.

"It's a biter," Kevin whispers, nudging my side with a grin.

I glance at him, noting the smile plastered on his face. He's taking all of this surprisingly well—almost too well—especially considering he lost his ex-wife and daughter only a few days ago. Some people process grief differently, I remind myself. But a flicker of unease settles in my chest. I'll have to keep an eye on him, just in case.

"Let's hang back, see where it goes. They're usually attracted to people," I say, my eyes locked on the slow-moving undead figure ahead.

We keep our distance, moving cautiously as it shuffles down the street. It doesn't take long before it veers off to the right, disappearing from view. Kevin and I exchange a quick glance, then move up the road, quickening our pace but keeping quiet. We reach the spot where it turned, and the sight that greets us makes Kevin's breath hitch.

"Holy shit," he mutters, his voice trembling slightly.

The biter had turned through the gates of a school, now slowly making its way into an expansive car park—the biggest school car park I've ever seen actually. But the real problem is what fills it. The entire area is swarming with shambling undead, their forms packed together in an eerie congregation. They're all gathered here, drawn to something, but what?

A chill runs down my spine as I take it in. The world fell apart in the early hours of Wednesday morning—school wouldn't have been open. There's no way all these people were just here, waiting. If they're all gathered, there must be a reason. Maybe there's someone inside. Amanda?

"Listen, Kevin," I say, tearing my gaze from the scene to look at him. "I'm not expecting you to come with me, but I need to take a closer look at that school. They're gathered there for a reason."

Kevin looks at me, his face pale, his brows furrowed. "You think your lady's in there, do you?"

"We're just friends... but yes, it's possible," I say, my voice cracking slightly as I speak. I feel the need to clarify, though I'm not sure why—it's not like it matters. My mind races as I scan the edges of the car park, trying to find a path that might let me get closer without drawing their attention.

I spot a gap between a hedgerow—just big enough to squeeze through. It'll lead me along the outer perimeter fence, but it should give me a better vantage point. Without hesitation, I start forward, crouching low. I glance back and see Kevin right behind me, his eyes fixed on the mass of dead beyond the gate.

A strange sense of relief washes over me. As much as I hate to admit it, having someone with me does make a difference. But I can't let myself grow complacent. If things go south, I hope I won't have to babysit him. Focus, Jack.

We make our way around the side of the school, taking it slow, careful not to make a sound. After a short walk, I spot a tree, its branches arching over the fence. It looks sturdy enough to climb—perfect for getting a good look at the main buildings and the windows. Maybe from up there, I can finally figure out what's drawing all these freaks here.

I nod towards the tree, giving Kevin a look that says, "Stay put." He nods in response, gripping his crowbar tighter, his eyes darting between me and the undead. Taking a deep breath, I start to climb, my fingers finding holds in the rough bark. As I pull myself up, I keep my focus on the task—one branch at a time—until I'm high enough to get a good view of the school grounds.

From up here, I scan the area, squinting at the rows of windows, searching for any sign of movement. Whoever, or whatever, is attracting the horde must be in there. The question is: do I want to find out what it is?

I keep scanning the windows, watching for any sign of movement, when suddenly the horde shifts—a ripple of agitation spreading through the mass of bodies. Something's riling them up near the far side of the main building. Before I can process it, I see a door burst open.

Three people rush out in a blink of an eye. The man in front swings something—maybe a bat, I can't tell—and two others follow close behind. One is small, a child maybe? The third is a woman with dark hair.

My eyes flash with both recognition and horror. I see the glint of metal as she swings towards the closest undead. Amanda.

A surge of panic shoots through me, and for a split second, I almost fling myself from the tree, over the fence, onto the patch of grass below. I stop, my heart pounding in my ears. It would be suicide—there must be a sea of at least three hundred corpses between me and her.

Every swing she takes, every step they retreat, I feel the tension tighten in my chest like a vice. They're trying to fight their way out, but before I can think, before I can shout down to Kevin or make any plan, the tide of undead surges, pushing them back. They retreat through the doorway they had just rushed out from.

Amanda makes it in first, the child right on her heels, then the man. I freeze in terror as I see something—something fast—moving through the horde. It weaves between the slower undead with a sickening grace, closing the distance towards the door.

A sprinter.

It lunges, launching itself at the man and child as they're about to cross the threshold.

"No!" The word rips itself from my throat before I can stop it, echoing out over the scene below. I see droves of the closest undead turn their heads, their empty eyes locking on my position. I don't care. My eyes are glued to the door.

Kevin shouts something up to me from his hiding spot, but it doesn't register. All I see is the sprinter. It reaches the child, ripping her from the man's grasp, her screams cutting through the moans and chaos. The man roars, his voice filled with pure desperation as he swings wildly, recklessly.

But it only takes seconds before he's overwhelmed—lost in a wall of hands and snapping jaws. The door slams shut behind them, leaving the man and the child out in the horde.

I sit there, frozen in the tree, numbness spreading through my limbs. I draw in a sharp breath, the air sticking in my throat, and all I can hear is the fading echo of their screams, swallowed by the endless moaning of the dead below.

Chapter 12

Amanda woke with a sudden jerk, her muscles stiff from a restless sleep in the armchair. The soft pre-dawn light filtered through the curtains, casting a pale glow across the small living room of the bungalow. Jack was asleep on the floor, a blanket of sweet wrappers covering him, his hand clenched around the handle of a mug. Amanda took a deep breath, closing her eyes for a moment. She could still see Oliver—his eyes dark and empty, his body lunging at Jack, her own hands bringing the katana down in one swift motion. It was too much. She needed to get out.

Careful not to make a sound, Amanda got to her feet, moving through the small space on light steps. Jack had saved her, in a way. He gave her purpose—something she hadn't felt in so long. But after what happened to Oliver, after what she did, what she had to do, she needed space. She wasn't leaving Jack, not for good. She just needed some air, some time to think, to clear her head.

She picked up her katana, still stained with Oliver's blood, and quietly slipped through the door, leaving the bungalow behind. As she walked down the narrow road, her breath visible in the unusually cold morning air, Amanda felt an odd mix of guilt and relief. Guilt for leaving Jack, even temporarily, and relief for the silence, for the opportunity to process the horrors of the past few days without feeling like someone else's life depended on her clarity.

She wandered through the village, the morning light slowly brightening, the streets still eerily quiet. Every step echoed; every rustle of leaves felt amplified in the silence. The isolation was almost comforting—no expectations, no need to speak, no one to look at her with gratitude or worry. It was just her, her thoughts, and the vast emptiness of the village.

She didn't know where she was headed. She just wanted to move, to keep walking until she found a place where the shadows of what she had done didn't follow her. Maybe a place with answers. But that was when she heard it—a faint sound, something out of place, drifting on the cold wind. A child's cry.

Amanda paused, her eyes narrowing as she tried to locate the source. It was distant, muffled, but unmistakable. The cry came again, clearer this time. Her heart clenched. Without thinking, she changed direction, her feet quickening, her katana in hand, the blade catching the early morning light. She didn't know what she would find, but she couldn't ignore the sound of a child in distress.

The cry led her to the edge of the village—a school, sprawling and dark, its gates open, as if beckoning her in. She could see the car park beyond the gates, a wide expanse filled with the dead, shuffling aimlessly, an eerie congregation of hollow-eyed corpses. They moved slowly, their focus scattered. But somewhere inside, Amanda was sure, there was someone alive. Someone needing help.

Amanda's breath caught in her throat as she took in the mass of undead, her pulse quickening. There must have been around fifty to one hundred of them all milling about, attracted to the cries. She could slip away now, turn back, find Jack, forget what she'd heard. But the child's cry echoed in her ears again, and something deep within her refused to walk away. She wasn't just fighting for herself, for Jack—she was still capable of doing good.

She gripped her katana tightly and moved to the side, avoiding the car park, searching for a way in. There had to be another entrance, somewhere quieter. The school was large, multiple buildings sprawling out with connecting walkways. Amanda found a service entrance to a building off to the right, a door slightly ajar, just beyond the line of sight of the gathered undead.

She slipped inside, the air cool and stale, the hallway dark. Her footsteps were light on the tiled floor, her ears straining for any noise beyond her own heartbeat. She passed classrooms frozen in time. Desks and chairs sat in neat rows, undisturbed by the end of the world with papers neatly piled on the teacher's desk.

The sound came again—a soft sob, echoing through the hallway. Amanda followed it, her heart pounding as she moved through the maze of corridors. She eventually reached a room, the door barricaded from the inside. She could hear muffled voices, the unmistakable sound of a child, a man's voice whispering hurried reassurances.

She knocked softly on the door, her voice low. "Hey, it's okay. I'm not one of them. I'm here to help."

There was a moment of silence before the barricade shifted, the door opening just enough for a face to peer out—tired, cautious eyes meeting hers. A man, in his thirties maybe, with a beard that looked like it hadn't been shaved since this all began. He glanced at her katana, then back at her.

"You alone?" he whispered.

Amanda nodded. "I heard the child... I couldn't just leave."

The man opened the door wider, revealing the small room behind him. A girl, maybe ten or eleven, sat on the floor, her knees pulled to her chest, her eyes wide with fear. Amanda stepped in, her heart softening at the sight. The man quickly shut the door behind her, shoving the barricade back into place.

"Thank you," the man said, his voice barely above a whisper. "We've been stuck here since yesterday. We'd heard there were people here and came to check it out."

Amanda nodded, taking a breath, her mind racing. She paced towards the window and closed it. Unfortunate that what led her to them, has also led the ravenous horde here too.

"We need to get out of here. There's someone I need to get back to, but I'll help you get out first."

The man looked at her, hope flickering in his eyes. "How? There's so many of them."

Amanda glanced towards the window, the mass of undead still shuffling aimlessly outside with more coming in through the open gates. She swallowed hard, her grip tightening on her katana. "We'll have to move fast. Find a way to distract them, create an opening."

The plan was rough, barely a plan at all, but it was something. They couldn't stay here—not with the dead gathering, their presence feeling like a tightening noose. She turned to the girl, her voice gentle. "Can you run? If we find an opening, can you stay close to us?"

The girl nodded, her eyes still wide, her lips pressed together in determination. Amanda smiled, offering a small bit of encouragement. "We'll get you out of here. I promise."

It was a promise she intended to keep. She had left Jack, needing to find herself again, to reclaim some semblance of control. And now, maybe, she'd found it. She would save them. She would make this right.

But as they made their way out of the room, the weight of the task ahead bore down on her. She knew she might not make it back to Jack. But she'd try. She'd do whatever it took.

Before either of them spoke again, a loud bang echoed throughout the empty school corridors. Amanda and the man looked at each other, concern etched into their faces.

Several thudding sounds resonated from the barricaded door to the classroom they were in.

"Damn. I mustn't have shut the door properly" Amanda admits, chastising herself internally.

The man glanced at the door, then back at Amanda, his eyes wide with fear. "What do we do?" he whispered, his voice trembling.

Amanda swallowed hard, focusing her mind. "They usually go away if we're quiet. We'll have to stay put for now—that's the only way out of this room." She explained the situation, but the words hurt her as much as they did them.

How long would they have to wait? Jack was no doubt awake by now, wondering where she was. Would he come looking for her? He owed her nothing.

Amanda, the man, and the little girl sat in silence throughout the day. As the light faded, the pounding on the door slowly stopped.

"Finally," the man whispered.

"Are they gone?" the little girl asked.

"For now," Amanda replied, trying to be reassuring without lying. "We'll have to wait until morning. Looks like the power is out—it'll be pitch black in the corridors."

"How do you know the power's out?" the man asked.

"The streetlights aren't on."

***

As the first light of day broke over the horizon, the undead resumed their assault on the door. It felt like they had been trying to lure them out all night—a deeply unsettling thought to Amanda.

"Let's give it a bit longer. If they're not gone in a few hours, we'll have to take our chances," Amanda said to the man, who looked less than pleased.

Without a better plan, he nodded, holding the little girl close.

"Where's Mum?" the girl asked.

The man looked up, his eyes wet with unshed tears, and shook his head.

"I'm sorry," Amanda whispered softly.

By midday, the undead were still pounding at the door. Enough was enough. Amanda had run out of patience, and, if she was honest, she was terrified of Jack moving on without her.

"Let's move," she said firmly, picking up her belongings.

"What do we do?" the man asked, his voice shaky.

"There's no time for doubt now. We need to move fast." She turned to them both. "Stay behind me. Stick close, and I'll get us out of here."

The man nodded, pulling the child close. Amanda faced the barricaded door, her heartbeat echoing in her ears as the pounding grew louder. She raised her katana, steadying herself.

"On my signal, we make for the hallway. I'll clear the way. Don't stop unless I do. Understand?" she whispered, her voice calm despite the turmoil inside.

The man nodded, fear and hope mingling in his eyes.

Amanda took a deep breath. "Ready... now!"

She turned the door handle before kicking it open. The door crashed against the wall, and two undead figures stumbled inside, their vacant eyes locking onto her. Without hesitation, she moved forward, her katana cutting through the neck of the first, then spinning to take down the second.

"Go!" she shouted, pushing the bodies aside and leading the way into the hallway. The man and the girl followed closely, their footsteps echoing against the walls.

More undead turned towards them, drawn by the noise, their guttural groans filling the narrow corridor. Amanda tightened her grip on the katana, guiding the group forward, her eyes darting from side to side, searching for a way out.

They moved quickly, Amanda cutting down any undead that strayed too close. The girl clung to the man, struggling to keep up as they pushed their way towards the side door Amanda remembered from before. The hallway stretched endlessly, every door revealing empty classrooms, every turn presenting more obstacles—more undead, drawn to their desperate flight.

Finally, they reached the door Amanda had been searching for, but it was closed. The undead must have already been inside.

Suddenly, an undead lunged from the side, crashing into Amanda and slamming her against the metal door, rattling it in its frame. The impact knocked the wind from her, leaving her struggling for a moment as the decaying creature clawed at her arm, pinning her against the door.

Then, a sharp crack echoed through the hallway. The man had grabbed a rounders bat from a nearby display case and swung, striking the undead squarely in the head. The blow staggered the creature, and Amanda didn't waste the opportunity. She shoved it back and swung her katana, the blade slicing clean through its skull. The body fell, leaving the hallway momentarily silent.

Amanda stood, breathing heavily, her chest rising and falling as she processed what had happened. She looked at the man, who still clung to the bat, his eyes wide with adrenaline—it reminded her of Jack. She gave him a nod of gratitude before turning her attention back to the task at hand. They needed to keep moving—now.

"Stay close," she whispered, taking a deep breath. She forced the door open, leading them into the open air. The car park lay before them, now teeming with far more undead than before. They were all looking their way already, sending a pang of fear through each of them.

Amanda led the way, her katana swinging at the nearest threats. The man followed, both of them fighting desperately as they pushed forward.

But they hadn't made it far, only a few metres before Amanda could see it was a suicide mission. The horde was enveloping them, closing in, cutting off escape routes.

"We need to head back! Back to the door!" She spun around, cutting down two undead that had moved to block their retreat.

They scrambled back towards the doorway, the dead closing in. Amanda threw herself through the door before turning to offer assistance to the other two.

It happened too fast. One moment they were there, the next they were consumed by the writhing wall of dead faces. She watched almost in slow motion as the young girl was snatched from her father's grip by a strange looking zombie. Its eyes weren't as hollow as the others, there was an intelligence written on its face, a thinking malice.

Before Amanda could react, the man—the girl's father—lunged into the crowd roaring fury and desperation.

There was another sound, something distant, different to the screaming and shouting that caught her ear before she slammed the door shut. Jack?

Printed in Great Britain
by Amazon